THE
STONE
OF
DAVID

LOUIS MICHAEL CORONA

Published by

Louis Michael Corona

Copyright © 2013 by **Louis Michael Corona** All rights reserved.

ISBN: 149054724X

ISBN 13: 9781490547244

This is a work of fiction. Names, characters, places, brands, media, and incidents are either the product of the author's imagination or are used fictitiously. The author acknowledges the trademarked status and trademark owners of various products referenced in this work of fiction, which have been used without permission. The publication/use of these trademarks is not authorized, associated with, or sponsored by the trademark owners.

To my wife Barbara who has stood by me through the years
and has always been the joy of my life.

ACKNOWLEDGEMENTS

My thanks to my children and family for their encouragement along with my neighbor and friend, Steve Ward, for his gracious support and guidance.

CHAPTER 1

❧

The young couple walked leisurely and haphazardly through the French Quarter. Jill was an excited tourist enjoying her second night in New Orleans. It was so different from her little hometown in Minnesota. Bobby had promised her a honeymoon she would never forget. A few drinks at the world famous Pat O'Brien's Bar made her a little light headed and a bit wobbly. Melancholy jazz music blared from the open door of a small café. It was an early summer evening, but already the infamous New Orleans humidity hung in the June air. Though the nighttime temperature was mild, there was little breeze to help cool the couple. They strolled from the bar to the Moonwalk bordering the Mississippi River only a few blocks away, but most knew, it was best to stick to heavily trafficked streets in the French Quarter. It might have been "The City That Care Forgot," but there were places in New Orleans that demanded great care.

"C'mon, let's walk through Pirate's Alley," Bobby said.

"I don't know if that's a good idea…looks kind of spooky," she whispered and shivered. Her mom had warned her about the muggings and murders. She saw something move across an opening between two buildings. "What's that?"

"Just an old bird, silly," Bobby laughed. "Don't be such a scaredy cat."

Looking for a short path to the river, Bobby led his new wife through Pirate's Alley bordering the St. Louis Cathedral. By day, the alley was a bustling throughway for tourists who made their way to Jackson Square where artists, street venders, mimes and horse drawn carriages all vied for the tourist dollar. By night, the dimly lit passage was isolated and foreboding, a place where a visitor or local passerby could sense both natural and supernatural danger in a city known for Voodoo and the occult.

A well-known and solitary lamppost stood sentinel midway down the cobblestone path. Pirate's Alley was rumored as a haven for slave trading and scoundrels in years gone by. Supposedly, it was also the stage for General Andrew Jackson's meetings with the Pirate Jean Lafitte. Though much of the alley's history was conjecture, the intrigue fit in well with the mystique of the Crescent City. The colorful and questionable past contributed to New Orleans legend and lore.

Bobby guided Jill to a bench alongside the ornate fencing of the Cathedral.

"Let's sit for awhile," he suggested.

"Are you sure… shouldn't we be heading back?" She looked around cautiously but saw no one.

"Why? We've got all night."

Jill began to relax a bit as Bobby encircled her with his strong arms and kissed her cheek. Images from their first night in the hotel consumed her, and she kissed him back. Lost in their passion, the world seemed to disappear. Suddenly, she came back to her senses when she felt something odd on her neck. She tried to ignore the sensation as she responded to Bobby's warm touch with a soft moan.

Then, there it was again…plink, plink, plink. *My God,* she thought, *there's something dripping from the top of the wall.*

"Bobby!" She pulled away hard and ran her hand along the back of her neck and hair.

Bobby stared at her with wide-eyed fright.

Confused, she looked at her hand. Even in the dim light of the lamppost, she could see it. Blood! They both jumped up and looked behind them at the same time. It was a body...slumped against the Cathedral fencing at the top of the stone wall. The eyes of the lifeless young man bugged out unnaturally and blood dripped from his nose.

Jill screamed from the depths of her soul before everything went blank.

Patrol Officer Mackey was first on the scene, but he quickly realized he needed to call in the big dogs. When backup arrived, they arrived in a big way. Representatives from the coroner's office, investigative bureau and the crime lab descended on the scene. What most surprised Mackey was the appearance of Lieutenant Ben Gervais accompanying Detective Inspectors Dampier and Harris from NOPD's Investigation and Support Bureau. Gervais wasn't predisposed to accompany his men on a field call like this.

"I hear we have a dead John Doe," said Gervais.

"That's right, Lieutenant," Mark Harris responded.

Typically, such a call would have been handled by the detective inspectors with no need for participation from the supervisor of the detective squad. Gervais was more than an asshole boss, he was a consummate politician. Recently, there had been an uptick in the city's violent crime statistics. Street drug trade was also becoming more accessible in tourist areas like the French Quarter. The city fathers understood that wasn't good for business, and Gervais was catching hell. Tourism remained a chief income producer for New Orleans, and they could not allow the overall safety of the city to come under fire.

Addressing the lab examiner directly, Gervais wasted little time taking charge.

"When did the subject expire?"

"The body is still in algor mortis," the examiner replied. "I would think less than two hours."

"What can you tell me about the cause of death?"

"I will need to run toxicology tests to confirm, but it looks like 25i."

"You need to be absolutely sure, damn it!" Gervais cringed. "The Mayor is all over the Chief about this 25i shit."

"I'm pretty sure, but I need to get the body to the…"

"Pretty sure won't cut it; you better be damn sure or you'll find your ass on the line."

Gervais was on the scene to deflect arrows and exercise damage control. New Orleans, like other metropolitan areas, was coping with an influx of synthetic drugs. As fast as NOPD could crack down on an epidemic of "spice," bath salts or other designer synthetics, a new and more dangerous concoction would emerge. 25i was just the latest, a liquid hallucinogen that could be dropped on the tongue with LSD like results.

"Problematically, 25i, or N-Bomb, as it is referred to on the street, is extremely potent and very unpredictable." The examiner breathlessly attempted to regain Gervais' trust. "The drug attaches itself to receptors in the brain, and there are extremely variable and potentially dire responses. Seizures, organ failure, paranoia and death are being seen in the city at an alarming rate."

"Thanks for the science lesson," Gervais barked, "but all I need is for you to make a conclusive determination and do it quickly." He turned towards the detectives. "Harris, does the vic have identification?"

"Wallet has an ID… a William Brewer. There's also a Tulane University student ID."

"Get the body to the coroner's office," Gervais shouted. "And in case you didn't hear me the first time, confirm the toxicology."

"Yes sir!" A chorus replied.

"Damn, another overdose, just what I need." Gervais slammed down his notepad. "Harris, notify the next of kin."

"Will do."

"See what you and that dipshit Dampier can do to unravel this mess." The irascible Gervais walked away muttering under his breath.

"What a friggin' butthole!" Dampier blustered. "Gervais rants and raves and we get the dirty work."

"Yeah, like informing the parents," Harris agreed.

⚜

The visit to Tom and Nancy Brewer's home was not an easy one for Ronnie Dampier and Mark Harris. Both were seasoned detectives. They knew New Orleans, and they knew its underbelly, including its narcotics trade. Harris, of Irish descent with wavy red hair, tended to be the more aggressive and assertive of the two. Though he was sometimes accused of a "no holds barred" approach to detective work, no one doubted his resolve.

Harris hated this part of his job, looking into the eyes of anguished parents who had lost their child was never easy. Any attempt at empathy somehow sounded remote and cold.

When the front door opened, Harris cleared his throat and coughed.

"Um…Mr. and Mrs. Brewer?"

"Yes?" Tom Brewer answered, looking confused.

"I'm sorry; we're here from the New Orleans Police Department." He showed his badge.

"Police? What's wrong?" Nancy Brewer pleaded.

"Unfortunately, we are here to inform you that your son was found in the French Quarter last night."

"Our son?" she gasped.

"Yes, I'm afraid the medical examiner believes he died from an overdose of a synthetic drug."

"Died? This can't be!" Tom shouted. "There must be some mistake."

"No, no, not Billy!" Nancy wailed and fell to her knees. Through tears she murmured, "Billy is a college student. He has a great future."

"I'm so very sorry for your loss," Harris replied. He felt like crap.

Harris had seen this many times before. At first there was disbelief, then anger and ultimately some form of resignation. The blood was completely drained from the startled faces of the parents. Dazed, they motioned the police detectives into their living room, while virtually collapsing on the sofa.

"We figured he might go out and have a few drinks from time to time," Nancy rambled. "We would not have been totally shocked by something like marijuana, but taking hardcore drugs? No, no, that defies what we know about our son."

"I understand your shock, Mrs. Brewer."

"How could you even begin to understand?" she snapped.

"Unfortunately, Ma'am, we are seeing an explosion of 25i in the city. It is a new hallucinogen... very unpredictable. Everyone reacts differently to it. How it got into your son's possession will be part of our investigation."

The distraught mom shook her head. "Please help us... get some answers. We've lost our... our only son."

"Hopefully," Harris replied, "we can retrace his activities. Do you have an idea who Billy might have been out with this evening?"

"We're not sure; he was not dating anybody seriously," Nancy said.

"Maybe it was a fraternity brother," Tom interjected. "He is a member of the Lambda Chi Chapter at Tulane. His closest friends are in the fraternity, and he spends a great deal of time with them."

The discussion went on for more than a few minutes, but it was all a blur to Tom and Nancy Brewer.

"I'm afraid you need to come to the coroner's office to positively ID the body," said Harris.

"Where is it?" Tom asked.

"It's on Martin Luther King Boulevard; here's the address."

Distraught, nervous and uncertain, with little idea what to do next, the first call they placed was to Nancy's brother, David Fournette.

⚜

There can be great power in evil. Historian and moralist, Lord Acton, said, "Power tends to corrupt, and absolute power corrupts absolutely." Yet biblical and historical events have shown that faith, perseverance, trust in God, and doing what is right, can overcome a superior adversary. "David put his hand into the bag and took out a stone, hurled it with the sling, and struck the Philistine on the forehead. The stone embedded itself in his brow, and he fell to the ground." (First Samuel 17:49)

David Fournette had never been the kind of man to shrink from a challenge, and in many respects, comparing him to the biblical David was not such a stretch. Nothing had ever been given to him, and he wanted it that way. He understood the concept of self reliance in a world that seemed to embrace the concept of getting something for nothing. If one hadn't known David well, underestimating him would have been easy to do.

David was the youngest of three New Orleans Police brothers. The ravages of Hurricane Katrina had claimed the life of his oldest brother, Tommy. It was not the storm's fury or subsequent massive flooding that took his life; it was his own NOPD issued Glock 22. The death, looting and inhumanity officers dealt with after Katrina generated post-traumatic stress disorder not unlike that experienced by battle-tested military personnel.

Tommy had been a decorated officer, husband and father of a teenage daughter. The family of police officers struggled knowing their athletic older brother must have felt hopeless as he tried to cope with the horrors he had seen during the aftermath of the hurricane.

David often anguished and wondered, *Could I have done more? Why didn't I see this coming?*

Though David was the youngest, the family often looked to him during times of sadness and turmoil. Their father had died of a stroke two years before Katrina, and their mom died six months after from pneumonia. But many in the family felt her death was caused as much by the death of her husband as from pneumonia.

David remembered what Tommy had said to him. "David, will you do Mom's eulogy? I don't think either Dan or I have the strength to do it." David was quick to accept the responsibility. Now his oldest brother was gone, victimized by his own hand. *If only I had been able to help Tommy cope with the trauma.*

David's other brother, Dan, fought through the dark days and institutional corruption of post Katrina and eventually landed as Assistant Commander in the Records Division. Though there were some elements of power brokering and intermittent requests to "modify" or "lose" records, basically this division was a safe haven from the rigors of the street and the seamy side of police work. Dan loved his family, but he and his wife had no children, and their lives were pretty much wrapped up in their jobs and each other.

David excelled in his New Orleans Police Academy training. There were always others who seemed more formidable candidates on the surface, but when the rigorous physical and mental testing was scored, David was always at or near the top. His training officer once told the squad, "David is like the thoroughbred… always closes from the rear. Just when you believe someone else has won the race, he comes out of nowhere to win the prize."

Many of David's peers also did well in training, but translating what they learned to the streets was an entirely different matter. When split second decision making and action were needed, David had the ability to deliver in spades.

After many commendations and a flawless record as a patrol officer, David landed a position as a detective in the Criminal Investigation Division probing serious crime inflicted on the law abiding citizens of New Orleans. Though his career had great potential, David struggled to get by Tommy's death, and the ongoing corruption and confusion of post Katrina haunted him.

He remembered the day he told his wife, "Honey, I'm going to make a change; I think I need to be in business for myself."

At some financial risk to himself, his wife Brenda, and two teenage sons, David decided he would hang out his own detective shingle where he could apply his ample intuition and persistence to solving the problems of others, unencumbered by the dysfunction existing in NOPD.

"This is a big step, hon," Brenda cautioned. "We have two children to educate."

"I know, Bren, but this is something I need to do. I want to be in a position where I can help people without all the police department protocol and bullshit."

His reputation helped acquire clients quickly, but only recently had he seen his income exceed police department wages.

David was not necessarily a physically imposing guy, standing 6'1" and weighing 180 pounds, but he worked hard at staying fit. As he turned forty-five, he knew a more balanced diet and consistent exercise program were his best defenses against the normal aging process. His curly brown hair, lean physique, fair complexion, and delicate facial features helped mask a toughness and steely resolve.

The call from Nancy hit David like a kick to his midsection.

"David, we've lost Billy," she cried. "We need you."

The words did not register immediately.

"What do you mean? Where are you? What happened?"

"Billy is dead. We're headed to the coroner's office. Please help us."

Shocked with disbelief, but remaining calm, David answered, "I'll meet you there."

As David arrived at the second floor coroner's observation room, he saw his sister and brother-in-law locked in an anguished embrace which barely held them from collapsing to the cold, grey, tile floor. Fraught with emotion, in a stream of conscious narrative, Nancy and Tom recounted what they had been told by the investigators. It was a horrid site. David had seen lots of dead bodies, but this was different, this was family. He felt physically nauseated.

"David," Nancy whimpered, "Billy wouldn't do drugs like this. Someone…somebody must've…"

"Somehow we'll get to the bottom of this, Sis." David stroked his sister's back, hoping to soothe her. "Do you know who's investigating for NOPD?"

"I have their cards…Mark Harris and Ronnie Dampier. I believe they are around here somewhere."

Though David had left the Department, he still held significant rapport with many of the city's finest. A glance back through the glass window of the morgue identification room disclosed Dampier and Harris. Both stood silently and looked somewhat surprised to see him. David excused himself and walked out of the icy room to visit with his past cohorts. After exchanging a quick greeting, David explained his relationship to the deceased victim.

"He was my nephew and a great kid. Have you learned anything more?"

"We have little in the way of leads," Harris reasoned. "But we do plan to talk to the president of Billy's fraternity to determine who might have been with him the night he overdosed. We're also checking his I-Phone texts to see what turns up."

"I'm certain Billy would not have willingly taken something like 25i," David said. "Someone exposed him to this, and I want to know who."

"Don't worry, David," Harris confirmed. "We'll find out who's behind this."

Left alone, with a moment of silence and time to reflect, David knew intuitively things were going to be extremely difficult for his family and for him personally.

Damn, what a waste! he thought. *And I wanted to be a PI. Never thought I'd be investigating my own nephew's death.*

CHAPTER 2

Harris and Dampier arrived at the fraternity house on Broadway at 9:00 a.m. the following day. It was already muggy; their damp shirts clung to their backs as they exited the nondescript Ford Taurus. *Damn New Orleans humidity,* Harris thought.

"Boy this Fraternity Row sure has some beautiful old homes," Dampier said.

"Not bad," Harris agreed. "Kids today got it good."

"They look like the mansions of the Uptown Garden District."

"Like I said...kids today." Harris thought of the rat-trap of an apartment where he lived during his tenure at the police academy. After eyeing a few empty beer bottles on the porch and weeds in the flower beds, the always practical Harris pointed out the trash.

"To bad they're too goddam lazy to clean up the place."

"Let's face it," Dampier replied, "guys are pigs."

"Come to think of it," said Harris, "at that age, all I had on my mind was women, drinking, and more women."

Dampier laughed.

As they approached the front porch, the door seemed to telepathically open, and a very well dressed young man walked out to greet them.

"You must be the detectives," he said. "My name is Mike Melancon, president of Lambda Chi. I also serve as Secretary for the Inter-fraternity Council." He pointed to the huge Greek letters on the side of the house. He appeared very bright and mature beyond his years.

This kid's got his shit together, Harris thought.

"Hello Mike, I'm Detective Dampier and this is Detective Harris."

"Very pleased to meet you both. We are all in shock, and shattered by Billy's death. Can you tell me what happened?"

"Thought we'd ask you the same thing," said Harris.

"Mike, do you know who Billy spent most of his time with?" Dampier began.

Without hesitation, Melancon replied, "John Cole."

"Cole?" said Harris.

"Yeah, John Cole…Architecture major just like Billy."

"Where would we find him?" Dampier asked.

"You won't have to look far," Melancon chuckled. "Probably still up in his room. Don't think he's left for class."

"Has he said anything about Billy?" Harris asked.

"No, but it's quite possible he might know something. He was close with Billy Brewer. I'd be happy to go get him, if you like."

"That would be great," Harris replied.

Within a few minutes, a clean cut, preppy young man strode toward the detectives.

"You guys…looking for…me?" he stuttered, holding out his hand.

Looks nervous, Harris thought. *Guess I would be too if my best friend turned up dead and two detectives were in my face…might take some prodding to get the real scoop.*

John Cole was a third year student at Tulane, not wealthy by any means, but with the well groomed looks, clothes and demeanor that allowed him to travel in well-to-do circles. There was some apprehension in his voice as he introduced himself.

"Billy…he's my best friend. I'm still having trouble believing he's gone."

"We understand; it's quite a shock," Harris said. "But we are here hoping you can help us better understand what happened last night."

"I'll…do my best."

It was apparent to Harris that John Cole hoped he would not be swept up in the investigation of Billy's death. Though he was not totally forthcoming at the beginning of the interview, he seemed truthful and admitted he was with Billy the prior evening.

"John, have you ever heard of 25i?" Dampier asked.

"No, what is it?"

"We need to determine how Billy might have been exposed to the synthetic drug 25i," Harris probed diligently.

"Drugs? I was with Billy the whole night. We were drinking, but I don't remember any drugs." He looked down at his shoes.

Bold-faced lie, Harris thought.

"Now, John, you need to think hard about this," Harris pushed. "Your friend is dead, and if you have information about a crime, you need to tell us. Withholding evidence would cause you a lot of problems."

Only after significant questioning were the detectives able to uncover the two friends had not only been together the prior night, they had also attended a private party in the French Quarter.

"An acquaintance of ours," the nervous young man sighed, "owns a house on Rue Orleans near its intersection with Rue Royal."

"Was that the location of the party?" Dampier pressed.

"Yes, we met this guy, Jim, a few months ago. He's got a lot of money; he and his dad own some sort of Import Company. His family is connected to very powerful and wealthy people."

"Go on, please," said Harris.

"He invited us to this party and we figured it would be a good time; you know, great looking girls…rich people?"

"Were there drugs at the party?" Harris asked.

"There was alcohol…" Cole hesitated. "After awhile Jim asked Billy if he wanted to try something different." His voice became more unsteady.

"And?" Harris prompted waving his right hand in a circle.

"He said it was some new type of LSD, but it wouldn't harm you. Said it would give you a great ride. Billy was reluctant, but said he would try it."

"What did you say?" said Dampier.

"I didn't say anything…it wasn't up to me."

"Please go on," Harris said, trying to get him back on track.

"Jim said the first hit would be free. If he liked it, there was more where that came from."

"How did he ingest the drug?"

"I believe Jim dropped some…on Billy's tongue…a few drops," Cole stumbled through the words.

"Then what happened?" Harris asked.

"I thought Billy was okay… uh…but in a few minutes he got very agitated and started acting weird. I couldn't reason with him; he insisted he was leaving the party. I got up to leave with him, but he pushed me away and ran out of the house. I had never seen Billy act like that. I was worried, but I never expected anything like this."

"Let me make sure I got this straight," Dampier said. "You saw this guy Jim drop some liquid on Billy's tongue."

"That's right, Detective Dampier," Cole confessed. He was visibly shaken. Undoubtedly, he felt remorse about the loss of his friend.

"Guys," Cole's voice dropped to a whisper, "this Jim can be nice when things go well, but if you cross him…all bets are off." He pulled his forefinger across his neck.

"I take it he has a bad temper," Harris said. "Can you give us a last name and address?"

"Not sure exactly…it's Marco…no Marsco…something like that. It's 201 Rue Orleans, and you are right about Jim's temper. I saw him strike a guy with a beer bottle when the guy accidently spilled a drink on his clothes. He wasn't sorry when he saw the cut on the guy's head, and blood all over his face. In fact, he seemed quite happy that he had hurt somebody."

"That's a big help," said Harris.

"What…whatever you do…you can't tell the guy I ratted him out…or I'll be dead too."

"Well, we need to pay this Jim a visit," Harris replied. "Don't worry, we'll keep your story quiet for now. It would be best if you have no contact with him until you hear from us."

"That's okay by me. I hope I never see the bastard again."

"We'll do our best to keep your name out of this," Harris assured. "But eventually we may find you are the only witness…the only one that can testify and tie Jim to Billy's overdose."

"Testify? Oh hell no! I don't want to testify; that's like putting a bull's-eye on my back."

"We'll see, hang in there," Harris said. "Thank you for your assistance."

Harris and Dampier quickly realized the location of the party house was only a few blocks away from the famous alley where Billy's body was found.

"The location of the cottage tends to corroborate the information John Cole gave us," Dampier said.

"That right," Harris told his partner. "And guess what? There's more. The automated City Directory indicates the house in question is owned by a Jim Marasco. Does the name sound familiar?"

"Marasco? Would he be related to Anthony Marasco a.k.a. Tony the Phony Marasco?"

"Ding, ding, ding, right again. Jim is none other than Tony's son," Harris chortled.

Tony was an importer, among other things, and a power broker in the city. You could not pick up the local paper without seeing the Marasco name on the business or society pages. Along with the well crafted image of Tony Marasco as a businessman and philanthropist, there were also underground rumblings that Tony and his family had ties to organized crime. Organized crime had changed in New Orleans. These were not the days of the flamboyant "Dons" who ruled their empires ruthlessly, and in fact, somewhat publically. Today, these crime lords used a much more sophisticated and private approach. Their legal businesses made money, but also fronted at times for more lucrative and illegal endeavors.

"Tony the Phony, huh?" Dampier looked worried. "That means trouble."

Anxious for an update, David Fournette made a call to the case investigators.

"What's up Harris? Any news?"

"Yeah, David, John Cole, Billy's best friend, tells us the 25i came from a Jim Marasco," Harris explained. "Said he gave the kid a free sample."

"Oh shit! Did I hear you say Marasco? Tony Marasco's son?"

"That's affirmative. This guy is no two-bit pusher."

"If the Marascos are involved, it'll make it doubly hard to get to the bottom of this."

"No shit, Shirlock!" Harris laughed.

"Justice will be no easy matter."

"But David, you know what they say, 'The bigger they come, the harder they fall.'"

"Yeah, right, right on top of us, like a giant elm tree. But wait, something doesn't add up. Maybe the kid is lying."

"What?"

"Well, why would Marasco OD the kid for free?" David pondered. "There's no money in killing your clients."

"I dunno," said Harris. "Maybe he's just a careless dumbass."

"Or a cold blooded killer. Anyway, we need another witness to corroborate Cole's story."

"Not we, David. It's up to NOPD to build a case that helps you get the justice your sister deserves."

"Well, if it is Marasco, there's no big mystery. We know who did the deed."

"Yeah, we know the perp…we just gotta figure out how to make him pay."

"I like the way you think, Harris."

Tony Marasco was not only rich, he had other resources. His connections to Board members of the Port of New Orleans, big wigs with NOPD and City Hall were well chronicled, definitely a mover and shaker. One did not accuse his family of a crime and live to prove it.

David remembered an article about Tony Marasco. *This guy has his grubby fingers in a lot of pies…probably city elite in his back pocket, as well.*

"Harris, you do know there will be repercussions from the investigation?"

"We fully expect it."

"If you even mention Marasco, Gervais will shit a brick!"

"Well, I don't know…"

"Harris," David interrupted, "he'll have none of it. Maybe you better let me do it on the sly. Jim will be lawyered up."

"But you…"

"I can help you get to this guy."

"It's too personal for you," Harris argued. "You can't be objective. Involving a P.I., especially one with connections to the decedent's family, will bring down even more pressure from the top honchos."

"Okay, okay. For now I will 'officially' stay out of it…but don't expect me to sit back on my haunches forever."

"As long as we know nothing, we can live with it," Harris affirmed. "Just don't get in our way."

"Good luck, you're gonna need it."

The visit to the expensive and well kept Creole Cottage on Rue Orleans was indeed a short one. A beautiful carved door greeted the two men as they walked up the steps to the crisp, white painted dwelling with contrasting green shutters. Owning a home like this in the Quarter meant you had money, lots of it.

A knock at the front door brought a salutation from a tall, distinguished man.

"May I help you?" came the stern greeting, door slightly ajar. There were no pleasantries.

"We're from NOPD; my name is Detective Mark Harris." Both men presented their badges.

Totally expressionless, Mr. Stone-face remained silent.

"Well, we're here to talk with James Marasco," Dampier interjected.

"Why do you want to talk with Jim?"

"He may have information about the death of a young man who overdosed. We have reason to believe the event occurred at a party in this residence last night."

"Do you now?" the surely man hissed. "If you want to talk to Jim Marasco, speak to his lawyer; the name is on the card."

There was little left to say. Jim Marasco had lawyered up, just as David predicted. Harris knew the visit was over.

⚜

By the time David received a call from Harris about the stonewall tactics of the Marascos, the results had already reached Lieutenant Ben Gervais.

"Gervais," Harris said, "has instructed Dampier and me to take this one slow and cover our tracks. You know how that dick-head operates. He won't ruffle feathers."

"Surprise, surprise. What did you expect?" David asked. "He's in Marasco's pocket like everyone else."

"Sorry, buddy, the wheels are gonna turn slowly, if at all," Harris stated the obvious. "Dampier and I will go through the motions, round up some more witnesses, but there will be no support from the higher ups."

David had seen it coming. *If you want something done, you gotta do it yourself*, he concluded, thinking of his sister and his nephew. *I'm afraid it's up to me.*

There was no doubt in David's mind Billy had been given 25i by Jim Marasco. Proving it was another thing. Rich men like the Marascos didn't get their drugs off street corners. There had to be more to this story, and finding the source of the drugs was the best way to find out. His mind started ticking off the possibilities.

David felt restless that evening. He noticed Brenda eye him suspiciously. Curly raven hair, a lithe figure, and soft features, helped belie her toughness, both mental and physical. Through two children and a teaching career, Brenda maintained the face of a "cover-girl," and she still had that same appeal that drew David to her as a student at the University of New Orleans. Even as a young woman, Brenda showed more maturity than many of her friends. She balanced a full college workload and part time sales work at a woman's clothing store. She did all of that, while still managing to get her teaching degree in four years. Among her many talents, Brenda could read David Fournette like a book, and he knew it.

"David, I can see you're struggling with Billy's death. I know you want answers for Nancy, but you're human, you need time to mourn."

"I'm having trouble coming to grips with this. I know who's responsible, but they are untouchable."

"The police are looking into this, David. You have friends on the force. They'll figure it out."

"Unfortunately, the perps have important friends as well. Already, I sense an attempt to slow down the investigation."

"Power and politics," she offered. "It always comes down to that, doesn't it?"

I failed my brother, David's mind wandered. *I can't fail my sister and brother-in-law.* His body stiffened, and his mind grew somber. It was obvious; he was struggling with a difficult dilemma.

"Honey, let's head to bed," Brenda suggested. As she led David to their bedroom, she seemed determined.

"Twist my arm," he snickered.

"Tonight it's up to me, David. Forget all this, at least for a little while."

Brenda seemed to know what David needed. They climbed under the covers of the king sized bed, and he felt his wife's supple body and comforting warmth against him. She drew closer, and David felt the tenderness of her lips on his mouth and neck. Her slow and rhythmic movements aroused him. He blotted out the worries of the world and gave in to his passions. He loved this woman more than anything else, and he loved making love to her.

For the briefest of time, his nephew's death and the Marasco problem seemed far away, but David knew he would soon have to confront his demons.

CHAPTER 3

David's Internet searches of "Marasco & Marasco" disclosed their major imports were olive oil, balsamic vinegar and wine. The business was conveniently located a few blocks from the Louisiana Avenue Terminal of the Port of New Orleans. With the assistance of an acquaintance who worked with the Port of New Orleans, David reviewed a copy of the Marasco files.

The records indicated the same port of call, carrier, agent and terminal were used for all Marasco shipments. The point of origin was the Italian port city, Genoa; the carrier, Italia Oceana, and the final destination, the Port's Louisiana Avenue Terminal. The schedule of shipments was monthly.

Nothing too unusual here, David thought.

At considerable personal risk, Rick Donner, his friend with the Port's European section was able to review the detailed manifest of Marasco shipments. Rick had asked David to call him anytime after 10:00 a.m. on his cell phone, so he could confidentially discuss the contents of the shipping logs.

At 10:01 David placed the call.

"Rick, this is David. Any interesting files?"

"Hi, David. I have been studying some manifests."

"Did you find any suspicious details regarding the Marasco shipments?"

"For obvious reasons…uh… I need to be careful with this, but I do see a few unusual items."

"Like what?"

"Well, the shipments do come in monthly; most of the shipments contain exactly the same number of shipping crates."

"Wow, that's exciting," David laughed. "Just kidding. You say most are exactly the same?"

"That's right, but every second shipment, without exception, contains ten extra shipping crates. There's probably a good reason, but it seems somewhat strange."

"Can you tell anything specific about the additional shipping crates?"

"Yeah," the somewhat nervous Donner said and paused. "Um…the quantities of wine and olive oil remain exactly the same, but the balsamic quantity is increased."

"That is interesting," replied David. "Any other unique aspects of the shipments?"

"Only one, they leave the terminal for various distribution points with one exception."

"And what's that?"

"The extra cases of balsamic are delivered directly to Marasco's business on Tchoupitoulas Street."

"Isn't that somewhat unusual for a national importer?" David asked. "Why would Marasco have the extra cases shipped directly to his business, and why only balsamic vinegar?"

"Hmm… don't know the answer to that one, my friend, but I have a hunch you'll be trying to find out."

"He must really like balsamic," David laughed again.

Rick Donner was TWIC credentialed which gave him access to tenant occupied maritime facilities, and the authority to escort others in port rented space.

"Rick, if the pattern holds true, next week's shipment will contain the extra cases. Do you think you could get me in to take a look?"

"Well, technically, you have no need to know."

"Use your imagination."

"How about a tour. Let's see, aren't you a potential customer?"

"Yeah, yeah, that's me," David snickered. "I'm thinking about getting into imports."

"But we will need to go through a fairly thorough clearance process."

"Look, Rick, how many more kids do you wanna see go down with 25i?"

"Okay, but you owe me."

"Give me a call when the next shipment arrives."

"Will do."

"I appreciate your help, buddy; this visit might give us some valuable information."

"Uh, that's okay. I think we can pull it off." Rick sounded like he was still trying to reassure himself.

"Later." David hung up.

David headed to the Irish Channel where Marasco's business was located. He understood his next mission was to find out as much as he could about Marasco & Marasco Importers. The Irish Channel was not so much Irish anymore. The working class neighborhood was now inhabited mostly by African Americans. Its name came from the Catholic Irish who settled in this area of New Orleans in the early 1800s. The "Channel" part of its name supposedly came from the low lying nature of the area that would flood periodically, but nobody knew for sure.

Wow! David was impressed. *The slums have seen a rebirth. More companies using the Port; residences remodeled.*

He circled the block of Tchoupitoulas Street and Jefferson Avenue in his 2012 dark blue Camaro SS. He had promised himself when he left NOPD he wasn't going to drive some standard issued, invisible, clunker. His heart yelled out for the Camaro ZL1 with a $60,000 price tag, but his brain pushed for the more reasonable SS.

Flying under the radar be dammed, he reflected. *I deserve this one luxury.*

Marasco & Marasco Importers was located in an attractive, well land-scaped, two story brick building with two metal storage buildings at the rear. The property was enclosed by a seven foot, chain-link fence with a barbed wire extension at the top.

Damn, balsamic vinegar must be like gold, David thought.

A small guardhouse stood right inside the automated gate. A sign on the fence read: "Private Property, Guard Dogs Present, Keep Out!"

Not too interested in receiving visitors, I guess.

A tall uniformed security guard stood on the curb outside the guardhouse smoking a cigarette.

During one pass, David noticed a neighboring warehouse positioned very close to Marasco's rear fence. Using it to gain entry was an option. The Dobermans and the guard, however, presented a significant obstacle.

Time to make friends with some Dobermans.

After a quick visit to a neighborhood butcher shop, David eased the Camaro around the block from Marasco's business and waited for the cover of darkness.

David walked nonchalantly through the driveway of the sheet metal company adjoining the rear of Marasco's property. The third quarter moon provided reasonable light, while high level cumulus clouds gave some cover.

With little difficulty, David was able to climb atop the roof of the sheet metal shop. Though he moved slowly with cat-like stealth, he could hear the two Dobermans running toward the rear fence. Black, swift-moving silhou-ettes were barely visible in the darkness.

"Here boys, come and get it," he whispered.

Not wanting to euthanize the dogs, David dropped chunks of chopped sir-loin, courtesy of the neighborhood butcher, over the fence. The meat contained a heavy dosage of acepromazine, which would sedate dogs rather quickly once ingested. The voracious animals were only too happy to comply.

Don't they ever feed these guys? he wondered.

As the dogs drunkenly sought a spot to rest, David threw a cloth over the barbed wire allowing him to climb down to the concrete pad outside Marasco's warehouse. He moved swiftly but silently along the side of the metal building. All windows of the structure were at least eight feet off the ground, and protected by metal bars. As he reached the front of the building, he could see the guard sitting in the guardhouse with his head down.

Probably reading the paper or playing on his I-Phone, he thought.

As he moved toward the large, reinforced metal doors of the warehouse, David observed an intricate fingerprint door-lock system, the type one might find in a Top Secret government facility or financial institution.

David shook his head and whispered, "Quite an intricate locking system for balsamic vinegar."

Getting into the building was going to be next to impossible. David moved a large crate below the front window of the warehouse and hoisted himself up. The crate shifted making a small scraping noise on the concrete almost causing him to lose his balance, but he managed to grab onto the metal bars.

Damn, that was close!

David steadied himself. With the assistance of the crate, he could just barely look though the bars covering the window. He saw a few crates of balsamic vinegar inside, but there were also a number of plain cardboard cartons and small plastic vials stacked nearby. The vials seemed to be empty, obviously intended for some future use.

"Funny way to distribute vinegar," he surmised.

Just as he began to focus on another assemblage of paraphernalia, without warning, the crate supporting him was yanked from under his feet. He fell against the building, and a quick glancing thud from a Billy Club struck the side of his head. Though stunned, David's police training and dexterity allowed him to place a round kick to the guard's solar plexus.

Reeling backward, a whoosh of air rushed from the man's lungs. The guard quickly gathered himself.

"You mine now you son of a bitch!" he shrieked.

Instantaneously, he lunged swinging his club. In a flash, David hooked the man's arm and drove his other forearm into the back of the man's elbow. The bloodcurdling crack of the elbow was followed by an ear-piercing cry of pain. In a split second, the application of a chokehold had rendered the man temporarily unconscious. David dropped him to the ground with a thud.

"Guess I'm not yours after all," he chuckled rubbing his head. "Sleep well."

Realizing the severely injured guard had probably hit the alarm, David hastened to the guard house, found the button for the automatic gate, and exited the premises.

As he entered the Camaro and sped away, he wondered just what was going on in that warehouse. Whatever it was, he felt certain it had something to do with his nephew's death.

⚜

As the guard awoke, he screamed in pain trying to straighten out his left arm. With great difficulty he called his boss' emergency line. He knew calling the police was not an option. Tony Marasco's men would see that he received medical attention.

"Mr. Tony…we had a break-in…over here at the warehouse. I almost got the guy, but he busted my elbow real bad."

"Break-in? Christ!" He wasn't pleased. "I'll send Gendusa over. Stay put, you little shit."

"Okay, Mr. Tony. Tell him to hurry. My arm's hurt…hurt bad."

Tony Marasco was pissed. His bodyguard, John Gendusa, went directly to the site and drilled the guard for more information, but darkness and the speed of the altercation allowed only a vague and useless description of the intruder.

Gendusa showed no sympathy. He kicked the man directly in his broken arm.

"Is that all you got, you worthless piece of shit?"

The guard cried out in pain and passed out.

Gendusa called his boss.

"Somebody put an ass-whippin' on Wilson. Severe fracture of the arm. From the look of it, the guy who did this knows how to handle himself."

"What about the Dobermans?" Tony asked.

"Again, no amateur. Came in here 'n' fed 'em somethin'. They're out cold."

"Dead?"

"No, still breathin'."

"Were my buildings broken into? Anything missing?"

"No, not that I can see. No entry. Maybe the guard interrupted him."

"Nothing taken, huh?"

"One more thing, Boss, the guard told me he surprised the guy while he was standing on a crate... seems he was tryin' to look inside."

"Thanks, John. We'll talk tomorrow."

"Yes, sir."

"I don't like the smell," said Marasco. "Somebody goes to a lotta trouble just to snoop around? Doesn't make sense."

Tony Marasco sat in his plush office at his uptown residence talking to himself, "I've had this location for over fifteen years with not so much as a single broken window. Now this goddam shit! Gotta get to the bottom of this."

CHAPTER 4

David hated funerals.

It was a sad day for the Brewers and Fournettes. Five days after his death, Billy Brewer was laid to rest at Lake Lawn Metairie Funeral Home and Cemetery on Pontchartrain Boulevard. There had been no traditional "Wake" the evening before. The Viewing and Funeral Service Mass were held the same day.

"We want to mourn Billy," Tom Brewer told David, "but Nancy and I can hardly find the strength to share our grief."

David understood. Socializing at an all night viewing, as was often the case in New Orleans, didn't seem appropriate for his nephew. Tom and Nancy Brewer had lost their only child, and their pain was excruciating. Nancy had said burying her son as soon as possible was the only way she could cope.

The optometrist and his wife, the Brewers, lived in Old Metairie, fairly close to David and Brenda who had moved to Jefferson Parish after David left NOPD. David's mind wandered back to the time they had decided to move near his sister.

"Warn the neighborhood; the riff raff are moving in," David joked with his sister.

The news seemed to delight Nancy. Of her three brothers, she was always closest to David.

"What do you have in mind?" Nancy shot back. "Perhaps pink flamingos in the front yard."

"Not too sure about that, but do you think the neighbors would object to a giant yard sale."

"Don't expect me to let on that you're my brother."

It was always like that between the two of them. Neither was reluctant to playfully engage the other. They had that type of trust and support.

Old Metairie was a very nice community. There were many stately residences including Mission, Tudor, Colonial and French styles. Further adding to its allure, the neighborhood possessed a booming and eclectic business district with boutique shops, restaurants and coffee shops. Beautiful oak-lined streets only added to its charm.

David and Brenda used the money they received from his first big case to put a down payment on a smaller, but very attractive Colonial. They knew they would need to stay gainfully employed, if they were going to give the boys the type of neighborhood and education they desired.

As he and Brenda walked through the door of the Colonial with their real estate agent, David had exclaimed, "This is the one, Bren! Can't you see us living here?"

"Yes, if you can see us paying the mortgage," his wife had answered.

"Details, mere details, Bren. You know my motto: Where there's a will, there's a way."

"There's no resisting when you make up your mind."

"It's a go then, we'll make an offer," David had proclaimed.

Brenda was close to her sister-in-law, and living in the same neighborhood gave her the opportunity to draw on Nancy for friendship and support. Tom Brewer was a good husband and father, but he had always been somewhat of a stoic. Nancy was the coordinator of the household and the catalyst for their family's social activities.

The tragic event, however, had unleashed a torrent of emotion in Tom. David knew both had a long grieving period ahead, but he wondered how long it would be before his brother-in-law would be able to resume a semblance of normality. David noticed Nancy watching her husband as he removed his sun glasses and wiped his swollen eyes.

"Honey," Brenda said softly with her hand on David's arm, "I'm worried about Tom. He is really having trouble coping."

"Yeah, I noticed."

"Nancy is going through the same thing, but at least she'll talk about it."

"We just need to stay after him," said David. "This is not the time to give him space and hope he comes out of it on his own."

With a stab of pain, David thought about his brother Tommy, and his suicide. *I won't let something like that happen again.*

As they left the green and serenity of the cemetery and headed for their vehicle, Brenda talked with David.

"It is nice to see how many people are here. So many friends share this grief with our family."

"Yeah, I guess so," David answered skeptically.

"You guess? Didn't you see the employees from Tom's practice, members of their golf and tennis club, and Billy's fraternity brothers? Losing a fine young man in the prime of his life affects everyone."

"I understand, hon. It takes a tragedy like this for people to stop and show their true feelings, but as time passes people tend to forget."

"You won't forget." Brenda touched her husband's arm reassuringly.

As they drove in silence to his sister's home, David knew most of the mourners would be pushed by the crush of daily obligations to get back to their normal lives. That would not be the case for the Fournettes and the Brewers. Their loss and pain would never totally go away.

Things were not getting any easier for John Cole. He remained conflicted, but he knew his friend Billy deserved justice. He wanted to tell the truth about Billy's overdose, regardless of the ramifications. His parents had always taught him to stick by his principles.

When the going gets tough, he reasoned, *the tough get going.* On further thought he remembered a Bible verse from his younger days in Sunday school.

"The Lord will rescue me from every evil deed and bring me safely into his heavenly kingdom. To him be the glory forever and ever." (2 Timothy 4:18)

John Cole tried to get on with his life as well as he could. He attended classes, fraternity events and social outings. He missed Billy and wished they had never gone to Jim Marasco's party that night. He wasn't too surprised when the NOPD called.

"John, this is Detective Harris."

"Hi, Mr. Harris, nice to hear from you," he said, stretching the truth.

"I'm afraid it looks like we are going to need your assistance."

"In what way?"

"The potential for the Grand Jury to return an indictment rests with your testimony. You are the only cooperating witness who can implicate Jim Marasco," Harris explained.

"What? What about the other people at the party?"

"Dampier and I got a list, and we interviewed them all. Nobody will admit they saw anything."

"Geez, I guess they're smarter than me, smart enough to be scared."

"That may be part of it…but apparently only the three of you were sitting together when Jim offered the drug."

"So…I'm the one that's going to take the fall."

"I understand, John. You're concerned, but you can't let this guy skate."

Cole knew the implications and struggled everyday with the dilemma of doing what was right while worrying about putting his own life in peril. Recently there had been some hang-up calls on his I-Phone. He could hear the low, slow, breaths of the caller. He would answer, "Hello," but after a few seconds the line would go dead. The calls were untraceable coming from a blocked phone, most likely a burner. The ominous calls were making him edgy.

He had also received a handwritten note at the fraternity house. It was a brief message.

Think before you speak.

Cole was spooked but resolved to see this through. After all, he had introduced Billy to Jim Marasco. *If it weren't for me, Billy Brewer would still be alive.*

Tony Marasco rubbed his forehead. John Cole was not the only one who was anxious. At Marasco & Marasco Importers, Tony had a meeting with his son, Jim, and John Gendusa.

Jim and Tony were always finely manicured. Jim was dressed in a Ralph Lauren sports coat and driver loafers. His tall, trim frame and black, slick-backed hair helped convey his player image. His father, a robust man graying at the temples and a little paunch around the middle, preferred a more conservative grey worsted wool suit with Jacquard stitching. They both reeked of money.

"I know this guy," said Jim. "He's nothing more than a scared college punk."

"How well do you really know this kid," Tony asked, "and what he will or will not do?"

"He likes the good life," Jim speculated, "a two-bit social climber. He'll fold under pressure."

"Are you prepared to take that chance?" Tony asked. "We don't want no investigators and DA's in our business, not to mention the Feds."

Father and son talked through the various scenarios. Gendusa sat quietly, his large muscular frame dwarfing the conference room chair. As Tony's lieutenant, he had been with him for over twenty years. He not only provided the muscle from time to time, he had become his most trusted advisor. Gendusa had seen military combat, and killing was not foreign to him. His cold, dark-brown eyes seldom gave away his mood or intentions.

"What do you think, John?" Tony said, turning to Gendusa.

"I don't like leaving things to chance," he replied stoically. "But a direct hit on this kid is sure to raise questions."

"What are you suggesting?"

"It would be most unfortunate for him, but not so unfortunate for us, if he were to have, say, an accident."

"An accident, huh?"

Jim piped in, "I say we make one attempt to buy his ass off. If that don't work… kill the bastard and dump him in the swamp."

Tony pondered his options. The older man loved his son. He was proud of him. His good looks and "way with the ladies" were impressive. He could also be trusted to market the business. He knew people who were all too willing to pay big bucks for their product. Jim had a good head on his shoulders, but a hair-trigger temper could get him in trouble.

The thirty-two-year-old Jim Marasco had been a student at the University of Arizona, but too much partying and too little studying brought him back to New Orleans well short of a degree in Marketing. Adding a second Marasco name to the family business suited Tony just fine. He would not lose his son, and he resolved to do whatever was necessary to keep him from doing jail time.

"Then, it's settled," the old man pronounced. "Mr. Gendusa will alleviate our problem."

Gendusa excused himself, and got right to the job at hand. He had a cerebral side, not so much a pure intellect, but a cunning that allowed him to precisely plan any intended mayhem. The 6' 3", crew cut and square-jawed henchman had the brute strength to incapacitate most men, and possessed the resourcefulness to accomplish his goals anonymously. He also had the patience to strike at the most opportune time. But, in this case, time was of the essence.

Gendusa's military background taught him discipline and loyalty. First and foremost, his job was to protect the boss. Whatever mess Jim had made, Gendusa would do right by Tony, even if it meant putting his life on the line for his snot-nosed kid.

Since the day after Billy Brewer's death, John Cole felt he had company. As he went about his daily routine, there always seemed to be eyes on him. At times he was sure he was being followed. Every weekend he liked to gamble. Black Jack was a passion, and he usually won more than he lost.

Rather than go to the downtown Harrah's, Cole liked to take the twenty minute drive over to the Boom Town Casino in Harvey. One of his fraternity brothers lived there, and Cole would typically meet him at the casino, do some gambling, and then head back across the river to the fraternity house.

Reaching the West Bank casino was an easy drive on a Saturday night. After crossing the Mississippi River Bridge, Cole traveled the elevated West Bank expressway to the casino. He eased the grey 2005 Mustang GT into a parking spot in the garage around 7:00 p.m. After grabbing a sandwich with his friend, he spent an uneventful four hours at the Black Jack tables. The extra $100 in his pocket made it a reasonably profitable night.

"Better quit while I'm ahead," Cole flippantly remarked to his friend, Joe.

"Do you ever lose?" Joe's jealously showed.

"Aw! Not everybody can be a winner. You want the casino to go out of business?" Cole teased.

At 11:00 p.m. Cole told his friend goodbye and walked to his grey sports car. He looked around carefully to make sure he was alone. Feeling good about his winnings, he smiled. *Maybe my luck's about to change.* Speeding out of the parking lot and checking his rear-view mirror, he turned off Peter Road onto the expressway and eased the Mustang up to sixty miles-per-hour.

He was singing to the radio as he went over a long, elevated bridge. Out of nowhere, a dark colored SUV nearly sideswiped his left fender causing him to jerk the Mustang violently to the right toward the concrete guardrail. In an instant, he was airborne.

"Oh! Shit!" he cried as every inch of his body seized in panic.

John Cole's last act was the rapid movement of his foot to the totally unresponsive brake pedal. After the car flipped end over end, the violent crash came to rest at the crossing street below. The front end of the Mustang collapsed into the passenger compartment and caught fire. Nobody could have survived.

⚜

The Sunday edition of The Times Picayune unceremoniously chronicled the event.

"A twenty-one-year-old Tulane University student died after a violent crash at the entrance to the U.S. 90 elevated West Bank expressway late Saturday night. According to troopers, John Edward Cole was traveling east on U.S. 90 and lost control of his car. The vehicle struck the concrete guardrail at a high rate of speed, and death was instantaneous. The vehicle is undergoing further inspection since it apparently lost braking power due to a ruptured brake line."

The news of the fatal crash quickly reached David Fournette. He read the *Times Picayune* every morning at the breakfast table.

"My Lord," he said putting the paper down.

"What?" Brenda replied.

"John Cole, Billy's buddy, and the only witness to the OD, is dead."

"Dead? Oh my God!" She turned white as a ghost.

He read aloud, "Troopers responding to the gruesome fatality indicated there was little traffic on the expressway at that time of night and no known witnesses. He flipped his car over a bridge."

"David, do you think…"

"Of course, he was killed. I don't know how, but…"

"David, these guys mean business. You better…"

"Brake lines…they were cut. The vehicle was towed to a facility where it will undergo further tests."

David knew there would be a comprehensive, in-depth vehicle inspection, but figured the likely conclusion would be "malfunction due to brake line failure." There might be doubts in some quarters, but virtually zero likelihood this "accident" could be tied to the Marascos. John Cole had paid the ultimate price, because he possessed knowledge that could incriminate the son of a powerful crime boss.

Now, David thought, *two promising young men victimized by that bastard, Jim Marasco.*

Within two weeks of Cole's death, the New Orleans Grand Jury convened in the government's case against Jim Marasco. Jim and Tony met with their attorney, Jeremy Givens.

"How do you suggest we prepare?" Tony asked.

"No John Cole," Jim spouted, "no case, if you ask me."

"I'm not asking you. Don't interrupt."

"In a way," Givens said, "Jim's right. The government will have little in the way of proof without Cole's testimony."

"Will Jim need to testify?"

"I'd advise against it."

"Hell, I'll testify. These jerks got nothin' on me."

"That's the point!" Givens exclaimed. "If you testify, the prosecutor will push all your buttons in the hope you'll slip and make an incriminating statement."

Tony Marasco knew the score.

"You will not be testifying, Son. Our attorney knows best."

⚜

David waited outside during the entire proceeding with a feeling of dread.

The Grand Jury ruled in Marasco's favor. There was insufficient evidence that a negligent homicide had taken place. Harris and Dampier outlined the information they had developed to the Grand Jury, but without testimony from their only witness, there was no direct evidence linking Jim Marasco to the drugs that killed William Brewer.

There were only a few lines devoted to the case in the newspaper. Tony Marasco had urged "friends" in the press to minimize coverage, so as not to further tarnish the reputation of a "fine young businessman and civic leader."

David noticed only one field reporter from a local TV station bothered to ask Jim a question, as he and Tony left the Grand Jury room looking elated.

"Mr. Marasco, can you tell us why the prosecutor filed a case against you? Do you feel vindicated?"

Jim was about to fire back when Tony put his hand on his son's shoulder and shook his head.

Tony stared a hole through the reporter.

"My son is a successful businessman. Successful people are sometimes targeted for no good reason. My son has said all he has to say."

Once again, Tony Marasco's crime machine had defeated justice. The NOPD investigation of Billy Brewer's death was now closed. The evening of the Grand Jury decision David met with Harris at a small coffee house on St. Charles Avenue.

"What a crock!" Harris railed. "First, these sons-of-bitches cause a kid to OD, and then they sabotage the indictment by ordering a hit on the only witness."

"Well, that…"

"And I feel like shit, because I made the kid testify."

David felt his pain. He had seen many witnesses disappear over his career.

"Yeah, but the experts found Cole's death was caused by a vehicle malfunction. And the naive and unsuspecting public will buy it."

"David, this is bullshit! No way it was accidental!"

"You know it and I know it, but…"

"What a pisser… higher ups are telling me to get over it and get on with my normal caseload. As far as they're concerned, the system has spoken…no case against that bastard."

"Yeah, it sucks. Justice system failed. I know you did your best."

"That's little consolation," Harris said dejectedly.

"They won this round, but rest assured, this case is far from over."

"What do you mean, David?"

"I'm gonna stay on them like stink on shit!"

David and Harris walked out of the coffee house and stood on the sidewalk.

"Let me know what I can do," Harris said as he walked to his car. "Just keep a low profile. These guys will kill anyone who gets in their way."

Standing alone, David could feel his raging anger. He wanted revenge!

Marascos are not above the law, David swore. *These killings will not go unpunished.*

CHAPTER 5

David met Rick Donner near the entrance to the Louisiana Avenue Terminal at 4:45 p.m. He had received word the expected monthly shipment for Marasco & Marasco had been offloaded from an ocean going cargo vessel and removed from 20' shipping containers earlier in the day. All the reinforced crates containing the shipped goods were still at the terminal awaiting land shipping destinations.

"Rick, thanks for calling," David said, reaching out his hand for a vigorous handshake. "Can we get in?"

"Hi David, we'll need to check in with the security officer at the access station."

"Will he record IDs?"

"Yeah. He'll log us in so there's a record of our visit."

"That's fine, Rick."

"Also, the terminal is monitored by cameras. They'll have 'eyes' on us, so we'll need to be circumspect as we survey the area."

"Got it, Rick, I understand. We don't want to make it obvious we're focused on Marasco's goods."

"Right."

"Hopefully, we will still be able to get some idea what they're up to."

"Don't handle the goods," Donner cautioned. "If they find out I tampered with cargo, I'll be in hot water."

"But what if…"

"From security's perspective, I'm there only to provide a facility tour to a potential customer."

"Gotcha. I really appreciate this."

As they approached the gate, Donner flashed his TWIC credentials. The guard, somewhat bored but still following procedures, quickly confirmed Donner was on the escort approved list. He also asked to see David's identification and then recorded their information in his computer.

"Wha' do ah say is the reason for da visit?"

"Review Port facility capabilities with potential customer, an importer," Donner answered.

"Importer?" The guy looked David up and down.

"Mr. Fournette has a certain interest in using Port facilities. I am simply giving him an overview of the terminal."

"What if I need to contact you?" the guard inquired.

"I have my cell phone here…there's the number. Mr. Fournette will be with me at all times."

"Keep da phone on sose I can reach youse…if I needs to."

The guard surveyed the pair for a few seconds and recorded the nature of the visit.

"Come back through da gate when you finish, sose I can check youse off my list." He nodded and unceremoniously opened the gate to the Louisiana Avenue Terminal.

"Friendly guy, huh?" David laughed.

"Typical. Gate guards aren't the brightest bulbs in the box." Donner laughed too.

The two men strode through the facility leisurely, frequently stopping as Donner indiscriminately pointed out various features of the terminal. It took only about fifteen minutes to reach the temperature controlled area of the warehouse where the product in question was stored. There were four separate palletized stacks containing the Marasco shipment.

The wine, olive oil and balsamic groupings were stamped, "Bella Ballerina, Cortona, Italy," with descriptions of the contents prominently displayed. As unobtrusively as possible, they walked slowly to the ten cases earmarked for delivery to Marasco. In virtually all respects the packaging looked the same, but there was one exception. The olive oil ticketed for further distribution was described as Aceto Balsamica, while the product bound for Marasco was marked Condimento Balsamica.

As surreptitiously as possible, Fournette pulled his I-Phone from his coat pocket and captured an image of both labels. Clearly, the labeling was very specific and every effort had been made to avoid confusing the two products.

"I wonder what's different about Condimento Balsamica?" David questioned.

"I have no idea," Donner said, looking over his shoulder.

Not wanting to draw unwanted attention, Donner dropped his voice to a whisper.

"We shouldn't linger. Better start making our way back to the gate."

David saw the anxiety in his friend's eyes.

"Think I've seen enough." He looked around, then he raised his voice so he could be more easily heard. "These facilities are quite acceptable."

They walked back toward the dock entrance. The security guard checked them out with little fanfare. With an appreciative nod to the businesslike guard, David and Rick Donner departed the premises.

"Thanks again, Rick. The shipments were exactly what you said we'd find."

"That's okay, David. I sure hope it helps you."

"Damn, I wish we could have busted open those boxes."

"Yeah, me too."

"The ten cases of balsamic headed directly to Marasco's have a different product description. I need to find out more about it."

"I can tell you, David, I'm not the only one who has doubts about Tony Marasco. A number of my friends at the Port wonder about him, as well, and his business ethics."

"You know what they say, 'money talks'."

"That's right." Donner smiled tentatively. "But I can tell you, if this guy is dirty, his backers will desert him like rats fleeing a sinking ship."

"I dig the Port pun...intentional or not," David chuckled.

After returning to his vehicle, David pulled his I-Pad from the side of the Mustang's console and powered up the Internet. A quick Google of Aceto and Condimento helped differentiate between the two balsamic shipments. Aceto was produced through a more refined and lengthy process, yielding a darker, silkier and much more flavorful balsamic, while Condimento was a younger, less expensive class of vinegar, intended for usage in another combined product.

Still mulling what all this meant, David drove to the red brick, three story office building on Carrolton Avenue which housed Fournette Investigative Services. He walked the steps to the third floor rather than take the elevator and unlocked the door to Suite 305.

His office consisted of a small waiting room with two upholstered chairs and a desk. No one would mistake it for a silk-stocking lawyer's waiting room. The desk was bare, awaiting an occupant. In his mind, David couldn't justify a real, live receptionist. That would be his next investment when he hit that big case that was always just around the corner. For now his automated voice messaging system would suffice.

To the right of the waiting room was a short hallway with a small, nondescript restroom on the left and David's office at the end of the hall. He opened the glass-paneled door with caution. *You never know,* he thought. The fourteen by thirteen room certainly wasn't ostentatious, but it had a functional and comfortable quality that suited his purpose. Two chairs, two file cabinets, a credenza, and the crown jewel, his secondhand, cherry executive desk and chair comprised the furnishings.

David sat down at his desk and placed an international call to Cortona, Italy. It was just a hunch, but maybe Bella Ballerina Winery could give him some answers. A voice with an obvious Italian accent answered the phone in English.

"Bella Ballerina, how can ah I give you some help?"

"I would like some information on your balsamic vinegar," David inquired.

"Sure, what would you ah want to know?"

"I'm interested in your Condimento Balsamica," David replied.

"But signore, I am sorry, we do not sell Condimento, we sell Aceto, the purest qualita."

David hesitated but then went ahead and asked.

"Don't you have a customer in New Orleans that buys your Condimento, uh…Marasco and Marasco?"

There was a pregnant pause, followed by a convenient deterioration in the man's English language skills.

"Please a hold on…ahhh…I am a having trouble comprendere. I will see if someone else…ahhh…can ah help you."

After more than a few moments, another less cordial and more direct voice came on the line.

"This is Franco Romano. To whom am I talking?"

"Let's just say I'm someone with an interest in balsamic…the balsamic vinegar you are shipping to Tony Marasco."

With that David heard a low click, and the line went dead.

Seems I hit a nerve…not real anxious to talk about the Marascos.

❧

David had indeed struck a nerve. Franco Romano was now on high alert. Bella Ballerina Winery was a profitable business, but not as profitable as the synthetic drug operation he had been running for the last five years. A number of people of the Cortona area knew Franco Romano was Mafiosi, but his relationship with the Polizia Municipale--the local police--sheltered him, and his winery holdings gave him both the money and protection he needed.

On the surface, the diminutive Romano was a jovial man. He liked to say, "I need to work hard; I have a moglie and six bambini to feed and clothe."

That wasn't too far from the truth. The balding Italian's stunning wife, Bella, the namesake of the winery, cost more to maintain than their six children combined. She no longer danced professionally, but she loved being part of Cortona's Alta Societa. Every eye turned when the svelte, 5' 10' raven-haired beauty made an appearance.

Bella had her act down to a science. All she had to do was bat her eyelashes and say, "Franco, I think I would look good for you in this new dress."

There was no resisting, because Romano knew she looked good no matter what she wore. He enjoyed his lifestyle and his wife. He didn't need any issues with his American business partner, and he certainly didn't need any problems with the Guardia de Finanza. The national police agency would not be inclined to look the other way, if they got wind of an illegal venture.

Don't like the sound of this, Romano reasoned. *This guy calls here... suspects something.*

He walked to the privacy of his office and picked up the phone. Eventually, the international connection was made.

"Tony...this is Franco. We have a problem."

"What is it, my friend?"

"Some guy...he called the winery today from your side of the ocean. Had some questions...the kind I do not want to answer."

"What?"

"Condimento."

"What about it?"

"Wanted to know about the Condimento…I shipped to Marascos. Talked to him myself."

"What was his name?" Tony asked calmly.

"Wouldn't say. But how did he know…"

"Not sure. A lot of people are snooping around lately."

"But somebody knows."

"How could that be?" Tony wondered aloud. "It comes right to my warehouse from the terminal where it is repackaged."

"I think you need to find out who this guy is."

"Thanks for the call. I'll get to the bottom of this. No need to worry, my friend."

⚜

Tony hung up the phone with a great deal of concern.

First the incident at the warehouse and now this shit, he thought. *Somebody's comin' after me.*

He had a feeling it had something to do with the death of the Tulane students. He immediately called his contact with the New Orleans Port Authority.

"Hello?"

"Henry, we need to check the logs at the Louisiana Avenue Terminal. I believe we may have had a visitor. Oh yeah, check the camera footage, too."

"Will do, Mr. Marasco! I'll get on it right away."

It did not take long for a Port marketing executive, a friend of Tony, to provide the information he needed. Tony, Jim and John Gendusa reviewed the prior day's Port records, which identified a David Fournette as an escorted visitor to the Louisiana Avenue Terminal. A Rick Donner provided the escort. Zooming in, the camera footage of the dock's temperature controlled area clearly showed a man photographing Marasco's shipment.

"That nosey son of a bitch!" Jim cursed aloud.

"No shit!" Gendusa agreed.

"Jim," said Tony, "see to it that the goods are moved to our facility, and don't waste no time. And make sure we have extra personnel on site twenty-four-seven."

He turned to Gendusa.

"John, find out everything you can about this Fournette character by the end of the day. I can smell it. That asshole is trouble."

Gendusa nodded and said, "I'll get it done, boss."

By the end of the day, Tony and Jim Marasco were reviewing a comprehensive file which Gendusa had placed on his boss' desk.

"Well, it appears Mr. Fournette is a private investigator," Tony said with a worried tone. "That's not all."

"What?" Jim sneered.

"He has a sister who recently sustained a death in the family."

Jim appeared uninterested.

"You wanna guess who?" Tony snapped.

"What do I care?"

"Maybe, you better care…it was Billy Brewer!"

"No shit. Billy Brewer?"

The father looked at his son with indignation.

"This is a dangerous situation, Son. We are facing a very skilled adversary."

"Fuck him!" Jim exclaimed.

"Fournete is no hired gun working for money. This is family. His family. This is personal."

"I bet he can eat a bullet…like anyone else."

"You better get out there, find out what's going on. And be careful."

Later as he sat alone in his office, the older Marasco sighed and shook his head. He knew his son had screwed up big time. Drugs were their business, but they were never to be personally involved in a drug transaction. Now, Jim's carelessness had exposed him to potential criminal prosecution and financial ruin. He rubbed his forehead hard trying to relieve the pain.

Fournette's bent on destroying everything I've built. He's crazy if he thinks I'm going to let that happen.

That very evening, workers at Marasco's facility repackaged the liquid contents of the Condimento shipment into amber, 30-milliliter bottles with dropper caps, the perfect size for distribution of 25i. Every bottle, with a street value of around $300, would leave the facility the next day, headed for their network. After paying Bella Ballerina and his other costs, Tony Marasco would clear around $600,000. He had two months before the next shipment of Condimento Balsamica would arrive in New Orleans. He needed to make sure David Fournette would not be an impediment to his cash flow.

CHAPTER 6

David knew men did stupid things when they were under pressure, or even when they were not under pressure. What he needed was a clever way to turn up the heat. Instead of simply focusing on the Marascos, he made a lot of noise with NOPD about the street sale of synthetic drugs, and 25i in particular. Still, David felt the police were slow to respond.

Time to shake the trees, he thought. *You know what they say, a picture is worth a thousand words.*

He worked tirelessly staking out well known street corners and captured plenty of footage of actual drug transactions. He also produced video clips of local cops driving right past drug dealers and prostitutes presumably on their way to the nearest donut shop. New Orleans news networks played the embarrassing videos over and over until citizen groups were outraged.

Though law enforcement was reluctant to directly implicate the Marascos, there was no denying the explosion of drugs in the city. And the inept attitude of authorities threatened to turn the city into a laughing stock.

David was proud of his sister. Nancy had written an op-ed in The Times Picayune imploring the police department to get off their asses and attack narcotics trafficking. The last line was sure to resonate with the citizen's of the city.

Don't let another young person die due to police inaction. We need to let drug dealers know they don't control our city--we do!

The threat of more and more bad publicity finally brought some action. City leadership did not want news of an epidemic of synthetic drugs splashed across the Associated Press. Tourism was their lifeblood.

"Your sister's piece made a difference," Harris told David. "Some of Gendusa's cronies are grousing...calling it a witch hunt."

"Guess Gervais is one of them?"

"No shit! Acting so sanctimonious...always covering his ass."

"This is only my opening shot...more to follow."

"Make 'em squeal, brother," Harris snickered.

David's relationship with FBI Assistant Special Agent Alan Smith also helped increase the pressure on the street. He knew evidence was lacking against the Marascos, but Smith agreed that police presence on the street would marginalize their distribution network.

"How can we get the public involved?" David asked of Smith.

"We've spent a lot of time cultivating Community Outreach programs," Smith offered. "Neighborhood Watch citizen networks have proved effective in crime prevention."

"So, the investment's paying off?"

"Yeah, once you get John Q Public involved, civic leaders and community organizers always follow."

"Makes sense," said David. "I'm sure they want to be viewed as leaders, not followers."

"True, their motives may be self centered, but they do help."

"We'll take any help regardless of the motive."

David shared what he knew about the Marascos with Smith. Both agreed it was premature to move directly on their enterprise. David hoped to flush them out by continuing to squeeze them at the point of sale.

"We need to choke off street trade," said David, "and harass the dealers."

"I agree," said Smith. "If the dealers are spooked, they might flip and identify the real money behind the operation."

"If we cut off the roots, the tree will die," David chuckled.

"That's right, but don't kid yourself, this tree will fight back. You better watch your back."

"I intend to."

"David, don't take this lightly. Marasco will sooner or later identify you as a problem, if he hasn't already."

"I'm counting on that," David said with confidence. "The more chances they take, the more room for a mistake."

Word spread like wildfire across the city. Every affluent user and two-bit junkie knew the heat was on. Given limited resources, special emphasis was placed on the $8^{th,}$ $6^{th,}$ $2^{nd,}$ 1st and 5th districts. From uptown to the Ninth Ward, undercover police and common citizen volunteers aggressively rooted out illegal drug activity. David watched the lead story on the 6:00 p.m. news.

"Are we turning the tide against illegal drugs?" the anchor pondered. "Local law enforcement agencies report drugs with a value of over $2 million were confiscated from the streets of New Orleans and surrounding parishes in the last two weeks. Further details during this evening's telecast."

If we keep this up, David thought, *we'll flush out the parasites, and the sooner the better.*

A call from Mark Harris was also encouraging.

"We must be putting a hurt on the Marascos," Harris said.

"Tell me more."

"I heard some of the guys in the 8th say their holding area looks like a pharmaceutical convention on the weekend. I'm liking the activity," Harris said playfully. "Hell, we'll probably get some push back from the parish prison, DA's office, and criminal court. No doubt they're gonna be hanging out the *No Vacancies* sign."

"All good," David agreed, "but has anyone fingered Marasco?"

"Not yet," Harris said, "it's like peeling back the layers of an onion."

"Can we peel a bit faster?"

David was pleased the all out frontal attack was making a dent in illicit drug trade. At the same time, he understood all too well, they might be hurting Marasco financially. *Only slightly wounded*, he thought. *I won't be happy until they're behind bars.*

The conversation at the Tchoupitoulas office was not pleasant. Jim Marasco flashed the anger he was known for.

"We can't sit still for this shit!" he shouted. "No doubt that two-bit dick is behind this."

"Where are you getting your information?" Tony asked.

"Our resources inside the police department say Fournette's pushing them…and the FBI hard."

"His sister's poison pen letter didn't help," added Gendusa.

Tony looked at the two men.

"So far this is a small setback. They don't have a single link to us. Their budgets and manpower will soon run thin, and things will get back to normal."

"Fournette is disrespecting us!" Jim was clearly pissed. "And we are losing our clout with our network."

"It's your job to control distribution," Tony snapped.

"It's not just the distributors," Jim said, "it's only a matter of time before we lose the confidence of the Capos and their soldiers. Fournette must be dealt with."

Tony Marasco's face became flushed and his posture more rigid.

"Your carelessness, partying and temper have already cost us greatly. Leave it to me to keep this organization in line."

"But…"

"No buts! No one, and I mean no one moves on Fournette until I say so. Am I clear?"

Jim nodded in silence, but he was not happy. He didn't like his ideas being disregarded, and he especially hated being dressed down by his farther in front of Gendusa. Gendusa paid him deference out of respect for the old man, but the younger Marasco felt an underlying resentment and lack of confidence from the Under Boss.

It was his ass on the line, and he was determined to show he had the ability to snuff out this threat. After the old man left his office, Jim went back in and removed a manila envelope from the top drawer of his father's desk. He walked back to his office to review its contents.

Gonna learn everything about this prick, he thought. *We'll see how he likes it when we bite back.*

Jim had promised his father not to make a move on Fournette, but he hadn't promised to stay away from his family. It was time that this thorn in his side knew the danger of messing with Jim Marasco.

While he plotted his next move, little did he know their Italian partner, Franco Romano, would soon begin to feel the simmering heat. DEA and FBI officials had given an initial alert to Europol and the Italian National Police. Historically, there was a reluctance to simply jump when the American authorities brought a potential drug operation to the attention of the Italians. Officials worried it could compromise their sovereignty. Politically, the Italian National Police wanted their government to know they were prepared and in control. Outside influence was considered a sign of weakness.

Less discussed, but also a consideration, was the potential they might accidentally flush out a target with highly placed political friends, further adding to the embarrassment of the National Police. Franco Romano was such a man.

David had a brainstorm. He and Alan Smith placed a call to Mario De Luca, Commissario Capo or Chief Commissioner of the Guardia di Finanza seeking his support. Hopefully, they could convince him to apply pressure directly on Bella Ballerina's operation.

"Hello, Commissioner De Luca, this is Assistant Special Agent Alan Smith with the FBI. One of my associates, David Fournette, is also on the call."

"What help can I give the FBI today?" the somewhat cynical Chief replied.

"We believe one of your citizens is providing synthetic drugs to an American associate. The guy's name is Franco Romano. He owns a place called Bella Ballerina Winery outside of Cortona."

"Well, Agent Smith, I have some concern. You say you believe…not you have proof."

"That's right, but…"

"This Franco Romano sounds like a man of some success. Such a man will have many amicos. Capiche?"

"Perhaps, we could ask you to provide more secretive support."

"What do you have in mind?"

David spoke up with urgency, "Increased controls on his business, more frequent government inspections and certifications, for starters."

"If this man is legitimate," De Luca said, "we could cause him to lose his business."

"If he's not legitimate, it would be a great embarrassment to the Italian authorities."

"I will give your request consideration," De Luca replied. "We don't want to make it easy on men doing bad things on Italian soil."

By squeezing Marasco's operations at home and abroad, David was certain they would react. He asked himself, *What would I do if I were in their shoes?* He didn't care to dwell on the answer.

Nancy Brewer struggled every day to bring some normalcy to her life. She tried to focus on her husband, hospital volunteer activities and simply being a housewife. But try as she might, during each lull in her activities, her thoughts would rush back to Billy's death. His passing had created a colossal void in her life and that of her husband. Tom had returned to work, but she found him detached. He was less inclined to go out, and seemed content to spend his evenings and free time at home. Having lost a major part of his life, he became overprotective of Nancy, calling her frequently and expressing trepidation at her outside activities.

In an attempt to keep her mind off her problems, Nancy met a friend for lunch at a little restaurant on Veteran's Memorial Highway. They each had a shrimp salad and a glass of wine.

Judy laughed, "I could have a few more glasses of wine, if we had the time. How about you?"

"I must admit," Nancy replied, "it does help me relax…and I need to do more of that." She remembered how much she had enjoyed small talk with Judy during happier times. Her long time friend and tennis partner had seemed worried about Nancy's health and the way she had withdrawn from her friends at the Metairie Golf and Tennis Club.

"I've got it," Judy said, "start playing doubles with me again. You enjoyed it so much, and everyone misses you."

"Thanks…for saying that, but I need…a little more time." Nancy felt mixed emotions.

"C'mon!"

"Tom and I are still in that phase where we find it too difficult to commit to outside activities. The hurt just seems to well up…no matter what we do."

"I understand, Nancy, but come back as soon as…well, as you feel you're able. You need to get your mind off of things." Judy paused. "Well, I need to make it to a dental appointment. I'll give you a call later this evening."

After saying goodbye to her friend, Nancy decided to go to the Lakeside Shopping Center near Macy's. After parking on the first floor of the garage, she walked across the walkway to the mall. Though there wasn't anything she specifically needed, it felt good to window shop and take her mind off her depression.

As she browsed the mall shops, Nancy had a weird feeling.

Somewhat lost in the moment, she made a small purchase at Williams Sonoma, and strolled back out to the mall concourse. Call it women's intuition or a sixth sense, but Nancy suddenly felt a strong sense of foreboding. She thought, *Better head home…what's wrong with me? I get spooked simply walking around the mall.* She chided herself and chalked up her trepidation to a general anxiety she had felt from time to time since Billy's death.

As she approached her Buick, she pressed the remote and heard the release of the door locks. She wasn't sure why, but she instinctively placed her thumb near the red panic button of the remote, again thinking she just had a case of the jitters.

She started the car, smiled, and promised herself she would take the Xanax her doctor had recently prescribed. She didn't particularly like the drugged feeling, but it did take the edge off her anxiety. She turned onto Bonnabel Blvd and headed to Old Metairie.

As Nancy neared Bonnabel's intersection with Metairie Road, a vehicle entered the road directly in front of her. She had to hit the brakes hard in order to avoid hitting the sedan.

"What a jackass!" she screamed.

She was used to New Orleans drivers. The aggressive vehicle stopped at the intersection waiting to make a right turn onto Metairie Road. As Nancy stopped behind the vehicle, she was instantly aware of a black GMC Yukon that nestled in behind her, inches from her rear bumper.

The front vehicle failed to move forward as traffic cleared, and instead it backed slowly into her. She also felt a jolt from the rear. *No happenstance,* she thought reaching for her cell to call 911. As quickly as the lead car struck her, it pulled away through the intersection. Nancy immediately accelerated through a right-hand turn and headed down Metairie Road. The GMC followed closely behind.

"Nine-one-one, what is your emergency?"

"My vehicle was struck!" she panted. "Two vehicles…sandwiched me in."

"What's your location, ma'am?"

"Traveling west on Metairie Road just past its intersection with Bonnabel. He's right on my tail!"

"I'll dispatch a vehicle. Is there a public place where you could pull over for assistance?"

"I think so, there's a restaurant up ahead…hurry, please hurry!"

Nancy knew the café just ahead had valet parking. She pulled her vehicle into the lot directly in front of the restaurant. As she looked to the left, she saw the tinted passenger side window of the SUV open slightly. A hand extended from the window, and Nancy could see the pistol's gleaming barrel. The passenger mimicked a shot by recoiling the gun's barrel, and then, the vehicle abruptly sped away.

Tom, David and Brenda made it to the scene almost as quickly as the Jefferson Parish police. Obviously shaken, Nancy could give only a general description of the vehicles. No one at the restaurant was able to get a tag number.

Tom seemed beside himself with apprehension. As he stood with Brenda and David, he vented. "I've already lost my son, and there is nothing we can do that will bring him back. I want justice, David, but I want my wife more. These people will kill us, if you don't back off."

David understood but tried his best to reason with his brother-in-law.

"None of us want to jeopardize our family. That's what these animals are banking on. This was an attempt to scare you."

"No shit. I'm scared!"

"No shots were fired, and that was intentional," David said calmly.

"No shots this time, but what about next time?"

"Tom, you have to…"

"David, they can get to us whenever they want. I can't lose someone else I love!"

David felt the pressure. He couldn't bear to see anything happen to his sister, but he also knew they would never be safe until the Marascos were behind bars.

CHAPTER 7

✠

The Fournettes entered St Catherine's for 10:00 a.m. Sunday Mass. When the boys were younger, Brenda and David had developed a somewhat lackadaisical approach to their Catholic Faith. It wasn't so much that they were disillusioned with the church. The perceived pressures of their lives had somehow helped them justify spotty church attendance.

When Rob entered kindergarten, Brenda felt it important that the boys practice their faith. She and David wanted both Rob and Tim to attend Catholic school. Many in New Orleans chose private school for their children due to the perceived academic inadequacies of the public school system, but Brenda was focused on the values and discipline a Catholic school education would provide.

"David, do you think we can swing it?"

"Swing what, Bren?"

"You know, we've been talking about sending the boys to Catholic school."

"I got a public school education and turned out okay, didn't I?"

"Things are different now."

"I know, I'm teasing. I want them to have every chance at success."

"I'm sure we can make it work," she said.

Though it was a significant financial strain, both of the boys were now enrolled in the all boys Jesuit High School. Sixteen-year-old Rob was a junior while Tim, two years younger, was entering his freshman year. David was fully supportive of this emphasis on their sons' education. He had to admit, at first, he looked at it as simply doing the right thing for his kids and Brenda, but over time had come to see the benefits to him as well.

David sat in church and tried to listen to the Priest's homily, but his mind wandered.

God, if you are ever going to give me guidance, I need it now. Please, God. Tom is fed up…wants me to butt out, but I know his fear is talking. Help me make the right choice; I need your guidance. Please!

David questioned his own judgment. He wondered if it was his false pride driving him to continue his crusade against the Marascos. Was his behavior self righteous? Did he persist in his quest because of his own self interest, while suppressing his concern for the safety of those so dear to him?

As if on cue, the congregation rose to hear the reading of the Gospel of Mark 4:35-41. The Calming of a Storm at Sea.

"A violent squall came up and waves were breaking over the boat, so that it was filling up. Jesus was in the stern, asleep on a cushion. They woke him and said to him, "Teacher, do you not care that we are perishing?" He woke up, rebuked the wind, and said to the sea, "Quiet! Be still!" The wind ceased and there was great calm. Then he asked them, "Why are you terrified? Do you not yet have faith?"

Indeed, David was facing his own personal storm. At times it seemed he was adrift in insurmountable waves, barely able to breathe as the raging swells relentlessly washed over him. Though the odds seemed overwhelming, David understood this was a test of his faith and fortitude. *I can't back off,* he thought. *So many others would be hurt.*

This was not the time to lose confidence and capitulate to his fear. David and his family stopped to talk with friends as they reached the church Sacristy. Apparently Brenda had noticed his distraction. When they were alone she tapped him on the shoulder.

"A penny for your thoughts?" Brenda took his hand. "Are you enlightened or perplexed?"

"Neither," David answered. "Just working through some things, I guess."

"It's Sunday," she said, "time to enjoy yourself."

"You couldn't be more right," he replied. "Let's go. I'm ready for some baseball."

They exited the church into the sparkling sunshine and cloudless blue sky. It would be a fine afternoon; they were heading to the new Jesuit baseball complex to take in Rob's game. He was the starting left fielder, and brother, Tim, was already showing his talents as a member of the JV baseball team. The boys were fine students, good athletes, and all around good kids. There was a lot to be thankful for. With his spirit rejuvenated, David smiled contentedly to himself.

⚜

That same morning over five thousand miles away, the Romano family and their American guest worshiped at the Church of Santa Maria delle Grazie on the outskirts of Cortona, Italy. Franco Romano, Bella, and the children were fixtures at the 16th century church. Much like the Etruscan walled city itself, the ancient church was steeped in history. The charm of the Tuscan town made it a natural setting for the novel, *Under the Tuscan Sun.*

The Romanos always occupied the same pew at the historical church which was built to house the miracle-performing image of the Blessed Virgin Mary. It was understood the front row pew was "reserved" for the Romano family. Their Sunday attendance had little to do with worship of God or devotion to the Catholic Church. The family's attendance and financial support were a critical component of their position in the town's hierarchy, and further legitimized Franco Romano as a pillar of the community.

There was no profound religious experience for Romano or his friend during the church services, nor was there any sudden thirst for absolution of their sins. They were quite content to maintain the illusion of piety, while embracing whatever evil was necessary to maintain their illegitimate and illegal gains. Synthetic drugs had proven highly profitable.

Romano turned to Tony Marasco.

"I am happy you have come to visit us."

Tony was truly happy to be in Italy,

"We have much to discuss, my friend, I must confess, I am most at home in the old country."

"Once Italiano, always Italiano, amico," Romano laughed.

"Yes, yes. Viva l'Italia." Both men laughed heartily.

That evening, the two sat on the vine-covered terrace of Romano's limestone villa.

"You have a beautiful place, Franco, and this Chianti is a perfect complement to the day." Tony toasted his friend.

"There is no place I would rather be at this time of the day."

"I can understand."

"Look at the setting sun and the serenity of the vineyards and olive groves." Romano waved his hand out toward the land. "I know I am a lucky man."

"Do not take it for granted, my friend. It's a wonderful feeling. Things seem to move slower here than in the States."

"I could not deal with that chaos," Romano said. "We have our problems in Italy, but they are small irritations I've learned to live with."

Tony was impressed by the opulence of Romano's lifestyle. There was something to be said for life in Tuscany. It was not like he didn't live the good life himself. He enjoyed the luxury and privacy of a gated home in the affluent Audubon neighborhood adjoining picturesque Audubon Park. He was indeed part of the New Orleans Elite.

Nevertheless, he felt more connected to his heritage in Italy. He loved the old world charm of Cortona, the medieval streets of the old town, its sidewalk cafes, and a morning cup of cappuccino. The beautiful rolling hills provided a stark contrast to the flat, and in some areas, sub-sea level streets of New Orleans.

"Speaking of problems," Romano asked, "what has happened with our inquisitive caller?"

"I'm sorry, mio fratelllo," Tony told his Italian "brother". "A foolish act by my son has exposed us to unwanted scrutiny."

"Is this man, Fournette, behind this?"

"Yes, but he is only a private investigator. He is pushing the cops to harass the street."

"That is not good for business," Romano replied waving his hands in frustration.

"I have many eyes on this David Fournette. He knows nothing that can hurt us right now."

"So far, I can handle the attention here amico, but what can you do to help me resume shipments of the 25i? I still have my production costs."

"Continue to ship on schedule," Tony said. "I feel the U.S. authorities will soon lose interest as cash and budgets get tight."

"You are sure...we can do this?"

"Si, time is on our side. If we play it smart, we will be okay."

"What about this Fournette? He is persistent. What is your long term solution to this problem?"

"Jim wants to move on him right away, but I fear this will make matters worse. Fournette has a lot of friends."

"Well, what then?"

"I also have friends."

"Yes?"

"I've told my son to maintain a distance for now. When the police are pressured to back off, he will not be much of a concern."

"I trust your judgment. I know you will not disappoint me. We will have a small glass of Grappa to celebrate your visit."

Tony Marasco and David Fournette were nothing alike, but they did have one thing in common: the hatred they felt for each other. On the same Sunday, five thousand miles apart, they both renewed their commitment to neutralize each other, no matter the consequences.

CHAPTER 8

It was like waving a red flag in front of the proverbial bull, when David Fournette confronted Jim Marasco in a French Quarter bar just off Bourbon Street.

Like most nights, Jim was out with his entourage barhopping. He never went out without four or five friends and a bodyguard around him. The young Marasco spent his time cozying up to the ladies. He had people to order his drinks; the most trusted carried his credit card to clear their tab. He was the "Alpha male," and his only job, as such, was to chase women. It wasn't like Jim Marasco wanted a strong connection or relationship with any of the woman he romanced. As with everything else in his life, he felt he could buy whatever he wanted. His good looks and deep pockets gave him all the advantages he needed to score.

"Party time!" Jim yelled as he entered the bar. "Lock up your daughters."

"Let the wenching begin!" howled one of the entourage.

"Give the barkeep my credit card?" He motioned to his bodyguard then turned to the bartender. "I need a Dewar's on the rocks, and keep them coming."

"You'll get a healthy tip, if you make it fast," Jim's arrogant lackey said.

This was Jim's style--let them know right away that it would rain money if they hung with him. He eyed two young women at the bar and pulled up a stool next to a tall blond.

Though it looked like the girl was barely of legal drinking age, she obviously had the attributes a man like Jim sought. Long, slender, toned legs extended from her short, red dress. Silky hair framed a flawless complexion and harmonious features that most men would find attractive. In other words, she was hot!

"How about a drink, babe?"

"Oh, I guess that'll be okay." She looked over his entourage. "You sure know how to enter a bar."

"Gotta let 'em know you're in the house. You from around here?"

"Hattiesburg...just visiting my friend."

"You sure do brighten up the place, honey. They're not kidding when they say Mississippi girls are foxes." Jim had the polish to exude charm, but just as it was with fine silver, the gleaming exterior could soon become tarnished, especially when he didn't get what he wanted.

After a few minutes, Jim's hand dropped to the young woman's knee then to her inner thigh as he leaned over close to her ear and he whispered, "What do ya say we go to my place?"

"And where would that be?"

"Right here in the Quarter, babe. Trust me, it'll be worth your while."

The girl suddenly appeared jittery. Her eyes shifted side to side, and she turned her legs away from him.

"Thanks, but my friend and I are just out having a few drinks. I have an early work day tomorrow, and we will be leaving soon."

"Come on!" he persisted. "You weren't in such a hurry when I was buyin' you drinks."

"I'm sorry but…"

"You think you're too good for me, is that it?"

"No, no, that's not it." She put a ten-dollar-bill on the bar, snapped her purse and slid off the stool. "Look, I don't want any trouble."

"You ain't leavin', I'm not finished talking to you!" He grabbed the girl's arm and spun her around.

The bar grew silent as all those nearby turned toward the commotion. With almost mystical speed, a man appeared out of nowhere and moved next to Jim Marasco.

"I don't think you want to do that," he said. "The lady said she was ready to leave."

Jim was pissed. He turned to stare down the intruder.

"Who are you to tell me what to do?" he screamed. "Oh it's you, Fournette."

Without thought Jim coiled to unleash a roundhouse punch to David's face. With cat-like reflexes, he intercepted the thrust in mid-flight. Just as quickly, Jim's bodyguard moved behind David encircling his neck with one forearm while applying tremendous pressure to the rear of his head with the other arm.

Years of academy training brought an instinctive response. David stepped backward with one foot and delivered a crushing heel-stomp to the man's instep. While simultaneously turning, he used one hand to turn the man and the other to deliver a crushing blow to his temple. The bodyguard immediately staggered backward, dazed, and stumbled in circles like a zombie.

Jim saw David motion for the frightened girl to leave the bar. He held his ground but David got right in his face. He could feel David's breath. He reached under his jacket for his weapon.

"Don't even think about it," David said.

"You think you're hot shit!" Jim yelled. "You're nothin' but a two-bit punk."

"Stay away from my family!" David shouted back. "You may think you're above the law, but you're not. Remember Billy Brewer and John Cole? You scumbag."

"Whatta you talkin' about? Don't threaten me."

"Don't like it, do you," David snarled, "when somebody fights back?"

"Just touch me...I'll see you brought up on assault charges. I got witnesses."

David turned to walk out the bar.

Jim pointed and spoke to nobody in particular, "A guy like that will find himself in deep shit, if he messes with the wrong people." He walked over and slapped his bodyguard across the face with all the force he could muster. "This is bullshit!"

Tim Fournette was settling in as a JV baseball player. The sandy haired fourteen-year-old had long, lean muscles, and at 5' 9" he was taller than 90% of the boys his age. At times, his growth seemed to sneak up on his 145 pounds, yielding short periods of awkwardness. By with a lot of practice, Tim quickly overcame these growth spurts, regained his muscle memory and increased his strength.

"Tim," David kidded his son, "I need a second job just to keep you in shoes."

Tim didn't think it was funny.

"Daaad, I can't help it."

"How about we give you some of Rob's hand-me-downs?"

"That's not fair! Rob get's the new stuff, and I get the rags."

"But, Son, we're not made of money."

Here comes the "money doesn't grow on trees" bit, Tim thought.

"How am I supposed to make the Major leagues without the right equipment?"

"You do know how to plead your case...just like you're mom," his dad relented with a laugh. "Guess we need to do what we can to help get your shot at the Majors."

Tim looked up to his father and older brother Rob. His dad had always supported him. He not only provided for the family, but he also made time for every important event in Tim's life. Tim knew his father had to work long and irregular hours. His mother told him so, all too often.

"Your dad is committed to helping people," she had said about a million times. "He's willing to be there for his clients whenever they need him. That's why he's successful."

For as long as Tim could remember, he was chasing his older brother, Rob. Like most younger brothers, he saw Rob's accomplishments and used them as a benchmark of his own success. Rob had more privileges due to his age, but he never let that keep him from being a real friend to Tim. Yes, there were the typical sibling rivalries from time to time, but when the chips were down, Tim knew he could count on Rob.

After having a driver's license for almost two years, his mom and dad finally bought Rob a used car. He had upheld the agreement that he could stay accident and ticket free for eighteen months. The metallic blue 2010 Chevy Cruze gave him some of the independence and status all teenagers crave, but it also provided some freedom from Mom and Dad. There was an understanding that Rob would be willing to chauffer his brother when Brenda and David were otherwise committed.

It was a mild, early-summer day when Tim was dropped off for afternoon practice by his brother.

"Thanks bro," Tim said. "Back at 5:30?"

"I'm going to visit a friend," Rob said, "but I'll be back."

"Okay, don't forget me." *It wouldn't be the first time,* Tim thought.

"Forget you? That would be easy to do."

"And don't make me stand around here waiting for you!" he shouted as the Cruze pulled from the parking lot.

Though the freshman third baseman had only known his teammates for a short while, his baseball skills, all around smarts, and sense of humor had already made Tim popular with the other boys. He felt exhausted, happy and relaxed as practice ended. He had cleanly fielded every ball hit his way, and for the most part, struck every pitch solidly during batting practice.

His cell phone rang.

"Hey Tim, it's Rob... I'm on my way..."

"Where the hell are you? It's 5:35."

"Traffic's real heavy. Be there in a few."

"But you promised..."

"Hold on to your panties...I'll be there!"

"How's Jenny? *Smooch, smooch, smooch,"* Tim said with disdain.

"Don't be such a comedian. On my way."

"No prob, see you in a few minutes," he responded and ended the call.

"Hey Tim, you need a ride?" one of his friends asked.

"No thanks," Tim replied. "My brother's on his way."

Most of the folks were gone when the grey panel-van pulled into the drive-through lane of the sports complex. Tim had been taught by his dad to be aware of his surroundings, but an untimely text from a friend caused him to adjust his tote bag on his shoulder and look down at the incoming message. Suddenly the van screeched to a halt right in front of him. In a split second the sliding door opened and two men wearing black hoods threw something over his head and muscled him into the van. He gasped for air in full panic mode as everything went black.

⚜

"Coach Smith, someone took Tim!" A teammate yelled.

"Stop! Stop!" Coach screamed chasing after the van and eating dust.

Breathlessly, Coach Andy Smith watched the vehicle disappear as he called 911. Another car pulled up nearby. The driver's side door flew open and Tim's brother popped out.

"What's going on? Where's Tim? What happened?"

Coach was on the phone, but a friend of Tim's replied pointing, "Two men pulled Tim into a van."

"Oh God! Oh God no! Where did they go?"

"That way…it happened so fast."

Rob wanted to go after them, but he wasn't sure what to do. He pulled out his cell phone and instinctively dialed his father.

"Hi Son, how's it going?"

"Dad, Dad…somebody pulled Tim into a van…"

"What?"

"… at the baseball complex. He's gone!"

"Gone?"

"Dad, get here as quick as you can."

"Are you sure?"

"Yeah, Coach called 911. Some of the players saw it. Should I go after them?"

"No, no, Son, stay right there. I'm on my way."

⚜

David drove at breakneck speed. It was only five minutes from his office to the sports complex. He arrived to a din of police cars and confused faces.

Jim Marasco! he thought. *I'll kill that bastard!*

It was too much for Rob. He was in tears.

"Why would anybody want to…take Tim?" Rob looked down at Tim's grey and blue tote bag on the grass near the curb. Leaning down to pick it up, he also found his phone. "Why, why Dad?"

"I don't know, Son?" David lied.

The suddenness of the abduction added to the chaos. Sifting through flustered and contradictory versions of what happened, they were able to uncover a few facts with reasonable certainty. The vehicle used in the kidnapping was a late model, grey Ford Van. Tim's coach was able to get a partial tag number. One witness who chased after the vehicle last saw it turning onto Airline Highway, heading west.

David sifted through the chaos of voices and sirens trying to stay focused on the information the police funneled to him. Rob sat sideways in the front seat of his car, his feet planted firmly on the parking lot surface. David could see the agony on his son's face and the tears streaming down his cheeks.

Brenda tried to console Rob, but all he could say was, "If only I had been here on time."

"It's not your fault," David said.

"Yes, it is!" he bawled, head in his hands.

"Do you have anyone in pursuit?" David implored the cop.

"Too late by the time we got here, but we issued an APB on the van."

David looked in every direction, as though he might see some invisible trail.

The police officer nudged David back to their conversation.

"Do you know who wud wanna hurt your son?"

Hurt my son? Hurt my son! the thought reverberated.

"Marasco," David replied.

"Who? Tony Marasco?"

"No, Jim, his son."

"And why wud he wanna do dat?"

"I've been working with law enforcement…to clamp down on street drugs. I had an altercation with a guy by the name of Jim Marasco in the French Quarter, just last night. He swore he would retaliate. I can't prove it, but I know his family is behind this."

"Has this Jim Marasco made any direct threats on you or your family?"

"Hell yes! Are you listening? He threatened me just last night in a bar. Witnesses everywhere."

"Well, I wudn't be so fast coming to conclusions."

David could see where this was headed. The Marascos were playing a "Teflon" game. None of this was going to stick directly to them. They would use others to accomplish their purposes, while protecting themselves from any culpability.

"You've got to do something fast, or..." David choked. He was beside himself.

The officer recorded the details and finally deduced the kidnapping met all the criteria for the Emergency Alert System. As an Amber Alert or child abduction incident, commercial radio, Internet, and satellite systems were mobilized. Electronic traffic signs on the roadway soon flashed messages describing the van and the details of the abduction.

Devastated, David fought back the urge to go after Jim Marasco and strangle him. His intellect and intuition threw up the caution flag.

Exactly what Marasco wants. If I make a direct move, I go to jail for assault. Or even worse, if he gives the order neither Brenda nor I will ever see Tim again. It was a sobering thought.

As he walked over to his family, David could see the excruciating fear in their eyes.

"What are we going to do?" Brenda cried. "They...have...our...son!"

David felt like shit. He should have anticipated this and provided some security for his kids.

"We will get him back, unharmed. I promise."

"It's my fault!" Rob sobbed.

"It is not your fault, dammit!" David shouted in frustration. "These are bad people. There was nothing you could do."

David tried to console his wife and son, but it was useless.

"Can't panic now, gotta focus," David spoke softly to himself. "Tim's life depends on it."

CHAPTER 9

Tony Marasco was in his office with John Gendusa going over his weekly schedule. His flat-screen was on the local WWL station turned up just loud enough for background noise. Abruptly, there was a break in the normal programming.

"We interrupt this telecast to inform you of an abduction of a fourteen-year-old, Caucasian male. Tim Fournette was captured by two men in black hoods from a baseball sports complex off of Airline Parkway. The vehicle believed to be involved in the kidnapping is a late model Ford Van with Louisiana plates ending in the numbers 4-1-2. If you see this van, do not take any action on your own. Please contact the police by calling 9-1-1."

"Son of a bitch!" Tony yelled at the top of his lungs. "Tim Fournette?"

The broadcast hit him like a thunderbolt, and his fury matched one in intensity. He heaved his coffee cup against the wall shattering it into a thousand pieces.

"My boy has defied me for the last time!" he screamed. "Did you know anything about this?"

"Hell no, Boss. I knew your orders, and followed them."

If this had been anyone other than Tony's only son, Gendusa would have already been given the order to eliminate him. There was no redemption from disloyalty or insubordination; even the best Capo or Soldier was expendable when the organization was at risk.

"John…any idea who took the boy…where he's being held?"

"I don't know shit," Gendusa responded. "Jim has gone completely off the grid on this one. Must be using only the closest members of his crew."

"He has created a problem for us with no good solution." Tony rubbed his forehead.

"There's always a solution, Boss. We'll find a way out."

"Does he actually think Fournette will make a deal to get his son back?"

"Wouldn't you?"

"Most men would be scared shitless worrying about their kid."

"Yeah, but Fournette…" Gendusa scratched his right ear.

"He won't back off until he has his son," Tony said. "And after he gets his son back, he'll still blow the lid off everything."

"Maybe we otta find out where Jim has put the boy."

"No shit. Get his ass in here!"

⚜

Lonnie Chambers' fishing camp was not what one would expect. This was no dilapidated, musty, run down shack. Many residents of South Louisiana treated hunting and fishing like a religion. To them Louisiana was "The Sportsman's Paradise." Many "camps" were owned by businessmen who utilized the elaborate retreats to entertain customers and employees as well as family. Chambers had always coveted one particular fishing camp. He was willing to live in a small, nondescript, poorly furnished house on the lam, but having a place where he could live the good life, away from the seedy underworld of his drug business, was always his plan.

A few years after Katrina, Chambers developed a beef with another dealer over "turf". He had lost one of his best street peddlers, when one of Malik Jones' men shot him and made off with $5,000 of his money. This was an affront Chambers could not overlook. Losing five Gs and one of his best street people was bad enough, but an attempt to put him out of business would not be tolerated.

Chambers instructed his men to canvas the streets and find "that son-of-a-bitch."

Malik Jones was not a guy who kept a low profile. Gold chains, diamond stud earrings, flat-billed cap and embroidered black tee shirt all provided the "bling" befitting an emerging force in the local drug trade.

"Hey, Lonnie, we found that shithead, Malik," his man said.

"Good news bro, where is he?"

"He been flashing a lot of scratch around town. We seen him go into a pad in Faubourg Marigney."

"Faubourg, huh? Pick me up…gonna teach that rat-bastard a lesson."

Chambers knew that surprise was a great advantage. He and four of his men burst in on the unsuspecting gangster and his crew as they were drinking and playing poker. Malik could only utter a few words.

"What the hell…"

"See yo' ass in the next life, you punk-bitch," Chambers yelled, firing a shot which struck Malik square in the forehead.

Chambers' men opened up and left no one standing. It was over in seconds.

"Search the place!" Chambers hollered. "I know this prick has money 'round someplace."

One of the men found a duffel bag jammed into a closet in the "shotgun" house.

"Shit, Boss, dis duffel stuffed with cash."

"Hand it to me."

"You gonna have a lot more than the five Gs this guy stole."

People like Malik didn't keep their money in the neighborhood bank, and the $150,000 they found was quite a bonus. Chambers walked away with a very nice down payment on the fish camp of his dreams.

Profitable day, Chambers thought. *Two-bit competitor dead and I get the dough. Thanks for the gift, Malik.*

David had seen a lot of strife in his life, but nothing like the kidnapping of his youngest son. It was so easy to advise other parents in this situation, but when it happened to him, the confusion and tension skyrocketed. The Fournette house was wrapped in a bundle of chaos and nerves. The FBI was now involved, as they were in all child abduction cases. Agent Alan Smith, a family friend, brought David and Brenda up to date.

"We've mobilized an FBI CARD team, that's Child Abduction Rapid Deployment. They have the expertise, experience and resources to thoroughly investigate a kidnapping like Tim's."

Brenda was too emotional to reply. She sniffled and wiped a steady stream of tears.

"I'll do whatever it takes," David said. "It's me they want."

"Your residence and cell phones are being monitored, and street teams are pursuing every lead that comes our way."

"Do you have anything credible to go on?" David asked.

"There are numerous 'sightings' of vans matching the description. Every lead is being followed, but at this point…nothing credible."

"What about Jim Marasco?"

"We pushed for a search warrant of his residence on Rue Orleans, but the judge had a tough time meeting the test of probable cause."

"I've got to be involved every step of the way, Alan. These assholes…the life of our kid is at stake."

"I understand, David. Just don't do anything stupid."

David stood up and walked to the window. He knew it was a waiting game. Unless they got lucky, nothing could be done until the perps called with demands. The thought of Tim being tied up in some rat infested hole made him sick to his stomach.

The gall of you bastards, David thought. *Give me an opening, and your ass is mine.*

Smith assured David that every move of Jim Marasco was being watched, but he had continued with his normal routine giving nothing obvious to use against him.

After many tense hours that seemed more like days, the phone rang at the Fournette residence. Everyone in the room jumped up and turned to the phone. Smith motioned to David to pick it up.

David walked slowly and deliberately to the phone and looked at the caller ID: *Unknown Caller.* When he picked it up, his heart pounded.

"Hello, this is David Fournette."

There was a short pause, and then a deep voice echoed, "You have created this problem. If you want your son to live, back off your crusade."

"I'll do what you want; just give me my son back," David said calmly, straining to control his voice. "Let me know what I need to…"

"Too early for that. Wanna see you sweat."

"Let the boy go. Take me instead, and your problem is over."

"We'll know soon enough, if you take us seriously."

"How do I know my son is alive?" The very thought made him gag.

There was a long pause, then something like a scratchy recording. "…Dad…they…got me…"

"You slimy…" David checked his tongue. He forced himself to calm down.

"We'll be back in touch." The phone abruptly disconnected.

David looked to Smith who was staring over the shoulder of another agent at his laptop.

"Payphone," Smith said. "Outskirts of town…eastside…two agents in pursuit."

"But the voice?"

"Voice modification," Smith replied.

David surmised his push against the street drug trade had ruffled Jim Marasco's feathers, and his son was paying the price. He tried to shake the vivid image from his mind.

Though the phones would continue to be monitored 24-7, neither David nor Smith expected a ransom call. This was not about money. The people who took Tim had other motives, like neutralizing David Fournette's aggressive tactics.

They had high hopes that Tim was alive and unhurt. Logic told David he was worth more to his abductors alive than dead. All their efforts were directed at finding the boy while still hoping they could flush out the Marascos.

The FBI provided protection for Rob and Brenda as unobtrusively as possible. It made it tough for Rob to maintain a normal life, but this was the only safe way for him to carry on with his activities. The family knew they needed to stick to a daily routine. Sitting by the phone waiting for a call was draining, and the pressure seemed to increase by the minute. Every day was a grind, but David resolved to keep his head and help his wife and son through the terrible ordeal.

When Jim Marasco showed up at the family business, he knew there would be consequences. Though his arrogance led him to believe his plan was working as intended, he knew disobeying his father would not be well received. There would be a price to pay.

As he entered the office, he saw his father talking to John Gendusa.

"What's up?" Jim said. He spoke as though he wanted to discuss a change in the company stationary.

Tony swiveled around to address his son.

"You…you have the balls to ask me, 'What's up?'"

"Somebody's in a bad mood." Jim tried to disarm him.

"I had to hear about this kidnapping…on a goddamned television alert? What in Christ's name were you thinking?"

Jim Marasco made the foolish mistake of challenging his father in a way few men would ever do. He remained defensive.

"You want me to take responsibility…so I made a decision."

"You call that…"

"Yeah, a good decision…while you wait around here and hope our problem will go away."

Jim sat down in one of the leather guest chairs facing his father's desk. He could see Tony's face turning red.

Tony shoved his executive chair back and walked around the desk. The older man did not move with the same speed he once had, but he was still a powerful force. He had been a Golden Gloves fighter in his youth, and he was no stranger to violence.

Jim tried to turn away when, without warning, the back of Tony's massive hand struck him across the face. The heavy chair rocked backward from the blow, and Jim barely stayed upright. He reeled in pain as blood poured from his upper lip over his new suit.

"You dare to disrespect me," Tony bellowed, "by coming in here like you are the boss of this family, and I am some kinda fool?"

Jim was at a loss for words. Finally he whimpered, "Is this the way you treat your only son?"

"You are only alive right now because you are my son. I sometimes ask myself if you could really be my son. Your stupidity and insolence can no longer be tolerated."

Jim looked at Gendusa, and he was sure he saw a brief smirk. There was no doubt how Gendusa felt. There would be no sympathy or support from him. He wiped his lip with a handkerchief he pulled from his coat pocket. Hanging his head, he stared at the carpet.

"So…would you kill…your own son?"

"You're not worth the price of a bullet," Tony added insult to injury.

"Well, what do you want me to do?"

The old man returned to his desk chair and leaned forward.

"You are going to tell us everything about this kidnapping. And then you are going to get out of the goddamned way, so this can be handled properly. Oh yeah, and by the way, if you ever defy me again, I will kill you…son or no son."

⚜

A businessman parked his vehicle in the self-park area of Louis Armstrong New Orleans International Airport and began walking to the terminal. He had heard the alerts about the kidnapping and internalized what the parents must be going through. He had two teenagers himself.

Five parking spots from where he exited his vehicle, he noticed a grey Ford Van. He looked at the rear license plate and noticed it was covered with a ragged piece of paper. Kneeling down and peeling the paper back, he could see the last three numbers: 4-1-2. He reached for his cell phone and called 9-1-1.

"Nine-one-one. Please state your emergency."

"I think you might want to get somebody out to the self-park area at Armstrong Airport."

"I repeat…what's your emergency?"

"There's a van out here matching the description of the one used in the abduction of the Fournette kid."

Authorities quickly arrived at the airport parking facility. The FBI and police immediately ran the plates, and found they were stolen. The identifying serial number had been filed from the vehicle. The vehicle was dusted for prints from top to bottom, but it had been scrubbed clean. This was no amateur job; someone with plenty of resources was responsible for this kidnapping.

David was called to the scene by Alan Smith. He knew the ditching of the vehicle must have happened quickly, because the first abduction alert went out within an hour of the incident. As he canvassed the parking lot, he noticed a security camera mounted on a nearby pole.

"Alan, look at that." David pointed. "Do you think we can get the footage from the day of the kidnapping? As best I can figure, the kidnappers made the switch around 5:00 p.m."

"It's quite possible. Let's visit with the parking lot management."

FBI personnel examined the camera footage from the day of the kidnapping. At exactly 5:15, the camera captured an image of a Black Suburban with heavily tinted windows stopping in the aisle at the rear of the grey van. The Suburban partially blocked the view of the occupants of both vehicles, but investigators could see two hooded men moving to the rear of the van and then to the side of the SUV.

They were half dragging and half pulling an adolescent clothed in a baseball practice uniform. Seeing the image of Tim, David felt an inexorable chill run through his entire body. This was not a chill one would feel on a frosty morning, but a wave of iciness that affects every fiber of one's being. *Oh God,* he thought.

Alan Smith broke the silence.

"Looks like Tim was unconscious."

"Sedated, so he wouldn't know where they were taking him," David answered in a low, subdued voice.

"That's my take on it too."

"Do we have any shots of the exit," David said, "to see if we can get plates on the SUV?"

"Yes, we do," a member of the CARD team responded. "Mississippi plates...we'll run 'um."

"Get an APB out on that vehicle right away," Smith ordered.

"Got it."

David figured the Suburban had long been abandoned or was parked somewhere where it would not be seen. Publicizing their knowledge of the vehicle switch had the potential to spook the people who had taken Tim. On the other hand, an announcement could help locate it. *What to do?* David pondered.

"Wait, Alan. Please keep this quiet for at least twenty-four hours," David asked.

"What gives?" Smith shot back. "Somebody might have seen the vehicle."

"We need to find the owner. If we find the owner…we find Tim."

"Okay, David, twenty-four hours. Let's see what we can learn about the Suburban, but then we go public. Sitting on this could backfire."

"Thanks. Let's get on it."

Nobody was more anxious than David to get his son back, but his experience told him to work the solid lead they already had before going on a potential wild goose chase. They surely would have to sift through many dead ends if a general alert went out to the public.

⚜

Jim Marasco knew he had to spill his guts. He had never seen his father this way without someone ending up dead.

"They have no clue where we're keeping the boy," Jim said.

"Where's the car you used to take the kid?" Gendusa asked.

"Ditched it…switched vehicles at Armstrong Airport."

"At the airport?" Tony shouted and waved his arms skyward. "You wanna be on Candid Camera?"

"Where are you holding him?" Gendusa spoke more calmly.

"That's the best part. He's in a remote fishing camp near Slidell."

"Slidell?"

"Yeah, right. It's not easy to find even when you know how to get there."

Slidell was a growing area somewhat isolated from East New Orleans by the eastern most part of Lake Pontchartrain. Access in or out of the city now necessitated use of the I-10 Twin Span Bridges. The bridges were built after

Hurricane Katrina had severely damaged the old trestle bridge and original Twin Span.

"Who owns the fishing camp?" Tony probed.

"Lonnie Chambers," Jim answered.

Tony and Gendusa knew Lonnie well. He was one of their key 25i distributors. He could move merchandise, but at times he could be reckless.

"Oh shit," Gendusa said nervously.

"Where is Lonnie now?" Tony asked. "Is he involved in holding the boy?"

"Probably at his house in New Orleans East. No, not involved, but he did provide the two cars."

"Boss, this guy is a loose end," Gendusa cautioned. "If the FBI finds him, he'll roll on us. I need to pay him a visit."

"Lonnie Chambers is one of our best pushers," Jim objected. "He brings in the money. Don't need to worry about him squealing."

"Everybody squeals…when their ass is on the line," Tony said. He turned to Gendusa. "Pay him a visit."

CHAPTER 10

David was driven to flush out the only lead they had. The 24 hour time clock was ticking.

The FBI ran the plates on the Black Suburban. It was a rental from A to Z Rental in Gulfport, Mississippi. Once a sleepy beach town, Gulfport had now become known as the Atlantic City of the Southeast. With the abundance of gambling casinos along the Mississippi Gulf Coast, the area also saw a burgeoning increase in restaurants, retail shops and other businesses like A to Z. I-10 allowed gamblers from the Southeast quick and easy access to upscale venues, and the economy was booming.

David reflected on all the changes.

"I remember when it took almost two hours to get to Gulfport from New Orleans."

"To travel sixty miles?" Alan Smith laughed.

"You took the Old 90 back then," David said. "Drawbridges, two lane roads, and red lights made it an ordeal."

"You would have made this trip if it took ten hours."

"You're right. I'd lose my sanity if I had to sit home wondering…" The words trailed off.

David had insisted he accompany the agents on the ride to the agency. The only thing keeping him from going crazy was his relentless drive to find his son. He sat in the passenger side of the modified, black Crown Victoria. As they exited the Twin Spans on I-10, little did they realize they were only a few miles from where Tim was being held. Sometimes, the answers that were right under your nose, seemed a million miles away.

"This is it," Smith said as they pulled into the A to Z parking lot.

"We don't have a lot of time," David's tone was urgent. "Let's go."

They arrived just before noon. The summer sun was already high in the sky, and there was only a slight Gulf breeze to combat the stifling heat. They walked through the front door into the cool of the air conditioned office.

Agent Smith tapped on the counter and showed his credentials.

"I need to speak with the manager."

The youthful desk clerk took one look at the three formidable looking men dressed in suits, and was all too happy to hand them off.

"Hey Lucas, you got visitors."

The manager came around the partition to meet the three men. The short man had a black comb-over and pencil-thin mustache, which gave him a somewhat comical appearance. He could easily have been the geek dispatched to one's house to scrub the family computer. His khaki pants and A to Z embroidered, sky-blue shirt gave him some semblance of legitimacy.

"How may I help you gentleman?"

"F-B-I…I'm agent Alan Smith."

"What's the problem?"

"We have reason to believe an SUV rented from this agency has been used in a kidnapping."

"Kidnapping?" Lucas turned white as a sheet.

"That's right, take a look at this."

Smith showed the manager a grainy picture they captured from the parking security camera near the New Orleans Airport. He handed him the license plate number.

"Hmmm," Lucas mulled, turning the picture sideways.

"Look familiar?"

"Yeah, that's one of ours."

"We need to know who rented it."

"Let me check." He reached over the desk clerk and typed in a few prompts. It took only a few seconds.

"Well?" Smith probed.

"The vehicle was rented eight days ago…due back yesterday. Nothing unusual. Renters often keep a vehicle a day or two longer."

"What ID do you have on the rental contract?" David interjected.

The geeky dude pushed the clerk aside and seemed to struggle to get out of his own way. He fumbled around poking at the computer keyboard.

"Pal, we're dealing with an urgent situation," David said angrily. "We need the ID!"

"Okay, okay gimme a second. Well, we have his credit card and a copy of his driver's license. Name on both is Jones.

"Jones? Are you sure?" David said sarcastically.

"Glad it wasn't Smith," Smith said, trying to get David to relax.

"Yeah," Lucas said, "a Thomas Jones."

"Tom Jones, very funny," Smith laughed. "Print me his info so we can run it."

The manager fumbled around as though he didn't know how to use the printer.

"C'mon, man!" David said in frustration. "We don't have all day."

"Okay, sir, I'm going as fast as I can."

Lucas' hands were shaking at this point. Apparently he wasn't used to the FBI breathing down his neck. He handed Smith the rental information.

Smith turned to his colleague, DuPont, and handed him the printout.

"Go get on the horn and find out everything you can about Jones and how we can find him."

It took only a few minutes for DuPont to get back to his boss. His FBI resources worked quickly.

"We've got a problem, Alan."

"What do ya mean, a problem?"

"A Mr. Jones reported the theft of his wallet to his credit card company and the police over a week ago."

"Let me guess, the card was lifted before the rental of the SUV," David said.

"Yeah, the credit card company is in the process of challenging A to Z's rental charge."

"Shit, we're starting over," Smith said, pounding his fist on the counter.

David was pissed; the rental agency had been duped allowing the kidnappers to get easy access to a vehicle. *Untraceable,* he thought.

"Lucas," Smith said, "looks like you got a problem; you have a rental fee you can't collect and a stolen SUV to boot. Don't you guys properly check ID?"

"We do…I'm not sure what happened. I don't know what to say."

David knew they would get nowhere beating up on the poor sap of a manager. He looked around the front office and spotted a camera behind the rental counter.

"Does that camera record all of your rental transactions?"

"Yes it does! Let's see, that was a while back. Might take me a few minutes, but I can get the image of that transaction." He hammered away on the keyboard.

"We don't have much time," Smith snapped. "A kid's life's at stake."

"Here it is," Lucas said, nervously turning the computer screen toward the men.

The likeness of the individual caught by the agency camera was only somewhat similar to Mr. Jones' driver's license picture. Unfortunately, a reasonable likeness was all it usually took to pull off a scam like this.

"We need a print of this guy's picture."

"Even better," Lucas said, "here's the address of the file."

"DuPont, get it to the FBI Facial Recognition data base."

"You got it."

David knew the image could be compared to the mug shots of over twelve million criminals. It was likely it wasn't this guy's first rodeo. There was a good chance he had been pinched before.

John Gendusa was getting sick and tired of cleaning up after Jim Marasco. He and two of his men pulled up to a brick ranch located a few blocks off of Bullard Road in New Orleans East. This area had experienced much devastation during Katrina, and there were still homes that were unoccupied or in various stages of renovation. Crime was not a stranger to this part of the city.

Lonnie Chambers could be a "loose cannon," but he was also a street-smart thug who would be wary of an unannounced visit from any of Tony Marasco's men, especially Gendusa. The driver made a few passes in front of the ranch. There was no sign of activity at any of the adjacent houses. The street behind his place had a number of vacant, overgrown lots, one of which was directly behind the brick home. The calculating Gendusa let the two men out at the rear lot.

"Get to the back door," Gendusa said. "Don't spook the guy, but be prepared if he tries to run."

"Got it, Boss!"

Gendusa drove around the block and parked across the street, two doors down from Chambers' place. He walked to the front door as casually as if he were a family member or an acquaintance. He punched the doorbell with his index finger.

The FBI Facial Recognition Unit delivered three possible matches to the image captured by the A to Z camera. The last known address of one of the men was Fort Lauderdale, Florida, while another was Tucson, Arizona. More promising was the third match, a Lonnie Chambers. The mug shot of a tall, skinny Caucasian man with a quirky smirk stared back at them. Thinning hair, a long neck and angular features were visible above a garish island print shirt.

David almost did a back-flip when he saw the man's address, New Orleans, Louisiana.

Smith read the arrest record.

"The guy's a local drug dealer, rap sheet as long as my arm. He's a little Houdini. Somehow, he always escapes a long incarceration, and he's back on the streets."

"Sounds like our man," David answered.

"Yeah, it would not be farfetched for a lowlife like this to have ties to Jim Marasco."

"What are his last street addresses?" David asked.

"There are two, both in New Orleans East. We'll need to check 'em out."

David knew they had to get to Lonnie Chambers fast, before the lead disappeared. He was their only hope for finding Tim.

"Let's go," David said.

They headed toward New Orleans East.

⚜

Gendusa heard footsteps and the front door cracked open slowly. When Lonnie Chambers eyed Gendusa, his body stiffened. He forced an awkward smile as Gendusa stuck his foot in the door.

"John, watta ya doin' here?"

"Tony is hoping you can help us…with some information."

Before Lonnie could say "come in" Gendusa muscled his way into the house. He motioned for the man to sit on the sofa and took a seat across from Chambers in a ratty club chair.

"I hear you may be helping Jim Marasco with a problem."

"Helpin' Jim? Watta ya mean?"

"I don't have time for this, dip shit. You know what I'm talking about."

"You mean the kidnapping of that kid?"

"What the fuck do you think I mean…helping Jim with his homework?"

"Didn't think I waz doin' nothin' wrong… I waz helpin' the Marascos, just like you."

"The senior Marasco was not made aware of this job, nor your assistance until it appeared on the news. He don't like surprises."

"How wud I know that? I didn't mean no harm. Look, I apologize. Jim told me he had his old man's blessin'. I didn't mean no disrespect."

Gendusa sat perfectly still and expressionless. His large arms rested on the side of the chair.

"So, I understand you got a vehicle for Jim, and he's using your fishing camp to hold the Fournette boy."

"Uh, that's right."

"Where did you get the vehicle?"

"Rented it using a credit card I stole. No worries…won't never be traced."

Gendusa remained stone-faced showing no visible emotion.

"What happens if it does get traced…back to you?"

Lonnie fidgeted, beads of perspiration formed on his upper lip. He wiped the back of his hand across his forehead.

"John, I need some water. How 'bout you, you need one? I can get it."

Gendusa shook his head negatively, but he did not speak.

Lonnie walked toward the kitchen located near the rear of the house. He opened one of the kitchen drawers and started to pull something out of it.

"I wouldn't do that if I were you," one of Gendusa's thugs said calmly.

Gendusa's two men had entered the kitchen from the rear with guns drawn and pointed at Lonnie Chambers. They marched him back into the living room. Gendusa was still sitting in the chair just as Lonnie had left him. The two men pushed Lonnie down on the stained, paisley-print sofa.

"Looks like tha scum meant to pull this on you, Mr. G." He held up Lonnie's 9mm Smith & Wesson.

"Lonnie, Lonnie you must have a guilty conscience," Gendusa said sarcastically. "Why else would you want to harm a visitor to your home?"

"John, don't kill me," he begged. "If you let me live, I swear, I'll protect the Marascos with my life."

The Capo spoke, "You don't know how right you are." He nodded to one of his men.

A single, silencer-muffled shot to the side of his head and the deed was done. Chambers slumped head first onto the carpet. His head twitched, blood spurting into the air.

The three men walked to their car and drove away.

⚜

After a futile trip to one of Chamber's last known addresses, the Crown Vic pulled up to the second. *This is our chance,* David thought. His heart pounded.

As they approached the door which was slightly ajar, they pulled their weapons. Moving cautiously through the passage, David saw the lifeless body of Lonnie Chambers slumped forward on the carpet. There was a single bullet hole through the right side of his head. A large pool of blood glistened as though it had only been there a few minutes.

Smith spoke in a voice barely above a whisper, "Make sure the rest of the house is clear." He holstered his weapon and looked at David in utter dismay.

"Shit! Shit!" David cried. "What will it take for us to get to these guys?"

"I'm guessing Lonnie outlived his usefulness to the Marascos," Smith stated the obvious.

"Dead people don't talk," David acknowledged. "We need to tear this place apart and see what we can find."

"Yeah," Smith agreed. "Maybe this dead man can talk."

CHAPTER 11

Tim Fournette had no idea where he was. The sharp smell of ether had rendered him totally unconscious as he was driven to God-knows-where.

The fishing camp was a perfect location to disappear. Land access was limited to a quarter-mile road of ground up oyster shells protected by a tubular steel swinging gate. Native pine, cypress, and oak trees provided maximum privacy. The back and west side of the camp were protected from Lake Pontchartrain by fifty yards of marshy shoreline, a covered boat dock, and a pine pier. A locked gate hindered any intruder from simply walking up to the camp from the dock.

Tim sat in the corner on the floor and took in his surroundings. The room was basically bare. It contained a lumpy mattress on the tile floor and a portable potty on the far side of the room. There was one window with thick metal bars protecting opaque wire-mesh glass. The steel door on the other side of the room remained locked. His captors slid food under the door through a small opening. He had literally seen no one in days. When he had first awoken from sedation, he went to the door and hit it as hard as he could with the palm of his hand. He pounded again and again, screaming in frustration.

"Who are you? What are you doing to me? Let me out of here!"

Nothing but silence in reply.

The ordeal was overwhelming. His first reaction was hysteria, then tears, then silent submission. He was alone and scared. For a long time it seemed he had been abandoned there, but eventually, a note was pushed under the steel door. It said simply, "No one can hear you. Shut up and you won't get hurt."

As Tim's crushing fear began to dull, his thoughts began to shift. He wondered why he had been taken. *Where am I? How can I get out of here?* Tim was never the type of kid prone to wildly varying emotions. He had the type of personality to analyze his problem and decide how best to handle it, the type of analytical thinking not commonly found in a fourteen-year-old. His mom used to kid him saying he was a lot like his dad.

His mind wandered. Though he was only fourteen, he had already experienced adversity in his young life. He remembered back when he was ten. He had sustained a severe break to his ankle in a little league game. There was concern not only that he would miss the season, but perhaps he might be limited in playing organized baseball.

The doctor explained there was potential for a loss in his range of motion, but David and Tim worked on the problem until Tim had fully recovered. It proved to him that giving up was not an option. *If you want something, you got to work for it,* he thought.

"Everybody gets knocked down, but winners get back up," his father always said.

Dad will find me, he thought. *Better chance of staying alive if I look like I'm cooperating.*

The long term quiet and the darkness were difficult to bear, but it also helped him focus when there was any sound at all. Mostly he heard muffled voices and footsteps from time to time. He could also hear the constant hum of the air conditioner followed by the quiet when the unit kicked off. The sounds seemed to fit a monotonous pattern.

On a less consistent basis, Tim would hear a distant whining sound. It would vary in intensity, progressively getting louder and then eventually diminishing until it was gone. There was some familiarity to the sound, but it was difficult to place. Suddenly Tim concluded, *A boat motor… it's a boat motor!*

David fumed with frustration.

Going through Chambers' house was painstaking. *Lonnie was never going to win any good housekeeping seal of approval,* David thought. Before they could really start digging, the FBI had to make sure the Coroner was called and the scene preserved for evidence. At the same time, David and Alan Smith flew through the place as quickly as possible to see if they could develop any clues as to where Tim might be held. It was like looking for a needle in a haystack.

"Damn, this guy's filing system is like a Rubik's Cube," David said in exasperation.

"Yeah, he's got crap stuffed everywhere," Smith laughed nervously. "He ought to be on that hoarding TV show."

"Why in the hell was he keeping these old Scratch-Offs?" David wondered. "This place is a mess."

"Pretty much lived off the grid; looks like he tried very hard not to leave any type of money or credit trail," one of the CARD members mused.

"Cash is king with a guy like Chambers," Smith replied flippantly. "Difficult to get credit when you would need to list your source of income as drug dealer."

David saw something in the messy stack of papers located on the night stand next to Chambers' bed.

"Look at this. It's a receipt for a safe deposit box." He held it up closer to read the fine print. "Community Bank One."

"Safe deposit box?" Smith said looking confused. "Chambers is the kind of guy that would keep his money under his mattress. What's he doing with a safe deposit box?"

"That's what I'm thinking," David said. "Must be something important."

"I'll get authorization to open it," said Smith.

"Do it fast. I've got to find my kid."

⚜

John Gendusa gave his boss an update.

"Chambers is out of the picture...got to him right before the feds."

"Where's the Suburban?"

"Stashed in the garage under the fishing camp...best to leave it there, too risky to move."

"The kid is still a problem. What do we do with him?" Tony asked.

"Need to make a decision. I'm sure the feds don't know where he's at, but we barely beat them to Lonnie."

"Do you trust the guys holding him?"

"They're two of Jim's best."

"This thing cannot be tied to us."

"I'm on it. I'll get 'em out if I feel they're gettin' close."

"Don't screw this up, John. Get their asses out before they connect this to us."

⚜

Armed with a warrant, Alan Smith and David showed up at Community Bank One. Though they were not in possession of a safe deposit key, they handed the bank manager a copy of the receipt and told her they needed the box opened immediately. After a quick phone call, she retrieved the keys for Box 156, and they walked into the limited access area. She leaned over, inserted both keys and slid the box from the bottom row.

When they first opened the extra large metal box, David was only mildly shocked to see two stacks of $100 bills two inches high.

"Damn," Smith said, "must be over 100k."

"Avoiding the IRS…or other thieves," David replied.

"What the hell," Smith laughed, "interest rates aren't so good anyway. What else do we have?"

"Birth certificate?" David mused. "Alonzo Paul Chambers, a fairly noble name for the degenerate Lonnie."

"Guess he had a mother once, who thought he'd amount to something."

"There's something else…look, a property deed!"

"Looks like Lonnie had an interest in real estate."

The legal description indicated it was a dwelling in an unincorporated area of Slidell in St Tammany Parish. The name of the grantee on the deed was an unusual one, Malik's Gift LLC. It made no sense to David, but a deed meant a location, and a location meant hope.

Eventually the government would be the recipient of Chambers' ill gotten gains, but, after a review of the contents in the safe deposit box, only the deed had the immediate potential to help find Tim. The question was, how was the late Alonzo Chambers connected to Malik's Gift LLC. The Louisiana Secretary of State's Office kept the filing information on all LLCs. A spot review of the corporate filing disclosed that the one in question was set up by one Alonzo Chambers.

"So typical of Chambers," Smith acknowledged. "He may not have been a rocket scientist, but he sure knew how to shield his assets."

"Too bad, his luck ran out," said David with a smirk. "I wonder why in the hell he named his LLC, Malik's Gift?"

"That's a story for another day," Smith answered shoving the copied information in his pocket. "Let's go take a look see."

CHAPTER 12

John Gendusa had covertly watched the recent moves of David Fournette. The trip to Community Bank One was not a good sign. He knew they were researching everything about Lonnie Chambers, and they seemed to be getting close. If they connected Fournette's kid to Chambers' property, all hell would break loose. *Time to make a decision Jim won't like*, he thought. He called Tony.

"Boss, we gotta make a move."

"What's going on?"

"The feds and Fournette have information about Lonnie's connection to the camp."

"Get Jim's men out, now!"

"Already underway; consider it done."

"No screw ups!" Tony yelled. "Everything's ridin' on this."

"They'll be no fuck-ups," Gendusa answered as he hung up the phone.

Gendusa mulled, *Too bad I can't eliminate the biggest fuck-up, Tony's asshole son.*

Based on the sound of muffled conversations, Tim felt there were probably two men holding him. He sensed a subtle difference in tones. His captors slid breakfast under the door as they did on prior mornings, but after that, their routine seemed to abruptly change. He detected a more frantic pace and the sounds of rushed voices. It sounded like the men were packing up.

He wondered if they were getting ready to move him. It frightened him that he might be drugged again and moved even farther away with less chance of being found. He had faith in his father's detective skills, but every day away from his family increased his concerns about being rescued.

God, let me get out of this alive, he prayed. He bit at his fingernails. *Where is Dad?*

Tim thought he heard the sound of an outboard engine revving close by. Within seconds, however, the sound trailed off and all he could hear was dead silence. Where did they go? Were others coming that might do him harm? It was hard for him to think straight.

The absence of sound seemed to flood Tim's other senses; the room appeared darker; he was more attuned to the damp, musty smell that penetrated his nostrils; and it seemed he could actually feel his fear as his heart raced and his palms began to sweat. It seemed like hours, but after only a few minutes the sounds returned more furiously than before.

Bang!

Oh my God, they're coming!

Tim's body seized in fright. He could hear running and then sudden stops. Doors were violently kicked open, and loud voices addressed each other in frantic tones.

There were sounds near the steel door. Tim moved against the back wall fearing the worst. Suddenly, there was a small explosion which knocked him to the floor, and the door was breached. Men armed with submachine guns and pistols came through the smoke. They stopped and scanned the room, and almost instantly he heard one of the men issue the order, "Stand down!"

As Tim cowered in the corner seized with panic, a large figure rushed over to him and said, "Relax kid. We're the FBI...Special Weapons and Tactical Team."

As he slowly opened his eyes, he could hardly believe what he saw.

"Dad!"

"Tim, Tim...you're safe now." David grabbed him and held him in a big bear-hug.

"Dad." It was all Tim could say.

"Thank you God!" David prayed aloud without shame. "Thank you for helping me find my son."

Tim tried to speak, but all he could do was sob. Finally, he got out a few words.

"I thought...I was never...going to see you...again."

Still holding his son, David said, "Did they hurt you?"

"I'm okay...I'm not hurt." Tim wondered about his mental health. The nightmares had been getting worse, but he said nothing. He was elated to be in the warmth of his father's arms.

Agents swept the house making sure no one was still on the property. One of the team members yelled, "Place is clear!"

All Tim wanted to do was go home, but he knew there would be a thousand questions. He tried to remember anything that might help the investigation.

"Tim," asked Agent Smith, "did you get a look at any of these people?"

"No, I was drugged. When I awoke, I was in this room. They never opened the door. Fed me by sliding the food under it." He pointed at the slot at the bottom of the busted door.

"When did they leave? How long were you left here alone?"

"Not very long, maybe fifteen minutes. I'm pretty sure I'm near the water. I heard the sounds of a boat."

"Left by boat, huh?" Smith asked rhetorically. "We musta just missed them."

"When you came…I was afraid…they were coming for me."

"You are near the water, Tim," David whispered. "That was very observant. Lake Pontchartrain backs up to this property."

"About all I could hear was the whining of a boat motor…from time to time…coming and going."

"You've been though a lot, Son. Let's get you home." David squeezed him so tightly he could hardly breathe. He looked toward Alan Smith and waved his head side to side, like, *No more questions*. "Your mom, your brother and I have been crazy with worry."

Tim felt tremendous relief as his dad walked him out into the sunlight. He could hardly believe how bright it was. Squinting his eyes, he tried to adjust. His dad handed him a cell phone.

"Call your mother; she needs to hear your voice."

⚜

Jim Marasco stood nervously next to his father. The news was not good.

At the same time Tim was being ushered from Lonnie Chambers' fishing camp, John Gendusa was providing an update over Tony Marasco's speaker phone.

"We barely got Jim's guys out in time. Feds are all over the place. Fournette too."

Jim bristled at the comment. He knew Gendusa was implying he'd fucked up.

"Why didn't you tell me…" Jim started to chide Gendusa before Tony cut him off.

"Shut up, Son."

"We gotta real mess here, Boss," Gendusa reported. "Not sure what they might find."

"I wanted to draw Fournette into the open, and get rid of him," Jim tried to explain his plan. "Now, I don't know."

Tony looked at Jim.

"They are very close to implicating us. If they had captured your guys..."

"Suspicions ain't proof," Jim said waving his hand dismissively.

"Listen," Gendusa said calmly, "all Fournette can prove is a two-bit drug dealer took his son."

"Motive?" Tony questioned.

"'Cause he was pushin' the feds to clamp down on the street."

"Do you really think Fournette will call off the dogs?" Jim said somewhat caustically.

"Fournette has his own pressures," Tony answered.

"Are we prepared to stop our shipments," Jim asked, "if they stay after Franco Romano?"

The old man looked like he was going to blow, then backed off.

"Fournette's wife has her son back," Tony said.

"But she also knows now what it is like to lose him," Jim countered.

"That's right," Gendusa said. "Fournette's entire family will be on his ass, begging him to leave this alone. I gotta admit that."

"What about the future shipments?" Jim asked again.

"I'll talk to Romano," Tony said, "and we'll arrive at a decision." He waved Jim toward the door. "Now, leave me and John alone."

Not wanting to challenge his father, Jim walked away. He knew he had been summarily dismissed. He seethed. Fournette had not only hindered his business, he had also caused a rift with his father like he had never seen before.

Jim Marasco felt cornered, but he was determined to fight back.

David relaxed for the first time in several days. He and Brenda sat with their children at the dinner table. She had cooked Tim's favorite meal: meatballs and spaghetti. Tim was still quiet; it was a lot for him to process.

"How about letting Tim do the blessing tonight?" David said.

"What a great idea," Brenda replied. "What do you think, Rob?"

"Guess so…it feels kinda good to have the twerp home," he said laughing.

"I guess you're up, Tim."

It was apparent Tim was starting to feel like his old self again as he said, "Dear Lord, thank you for bringing me home safe and sound…my parents need one good kid in the house."

They all laughed.

The evening meal at the Fournette's was as good as any David had ever tasted. Tim was home, and his brother was truly smiling for the first time in a week. David exchanged glances with his wife. Though she had never completely succumbed to the tremendous pressure she was under, he knew the weight of the world was lifted from her shoulders. Reveling in contentment, a pang of foreboding suddenly shot through David's midsection. Tim was home, but Billy would never be home. While David felt elation for his own family, Nancy never would.

Later that night, Alan Smith returned to the Fournette residence. He pledged there would be protection for David's family. The rest of his news was not as comforting.

"David, the Marascos remind me of Houdini."

"How so?" David answered while thinking, *This can't be good news.*

"Well, Jim Marasco skated on your nephew's homicide…and he escaped John Cole's, as well. Now, we have found no trail from Lonnie Chambers to the Marascos."

"What are you telling me, Alan?"

"We found no evidence at the fish camp connecting it to the Marascos."

"But Lonnie rented the car!"

"Yeah, but still, he's a dealer. Could have just been striking back at you."

"So that's it?" David could hardly believe what he was hearing.

"We'll keep up the street pressure…and watch for any shipment going into Marasco's warehouse…but, at present, we are basically stumped."

"What about ballistics…the weapon that killed Lonnie?"

"A dead end…uh…I'm not sure how much longer I can push the Bureau for resources."

"Don't give up on this, Pal, I need you. Tom and Nancy need you."

Smith rose and David walked him to the front door. He turned to David and said somewhat dejectedly, "I'm not giving up."

"Look, Alan. I got my son back, but I'm still not sleeping much."

"David, you may have to…"

"I won't rest until I see those bastards fry!"

"David, look, I'm your best friend so I can say this…you need to look out for your own family."

"You know me." It was all he said as he closed the door.

David couldn't get Billy out of his mind. The Marascos were still living the good life while his nephew was dead and his family traumatized. He tried to think clearly, devise a strategy, but he kept coming up blank.

He told his boys goodnight and went to his bedroom. Brenda was there waiting for him in one of her sexiest gowns. Though he was still troubled, he smiled and embraced her. For now, he would be thankful he had Brenda back, as well as his son.

CHAPTER 13

The news reports of Tim's release all trumpeted the same basic synopsis.

"A harrowing kidnapping was foiled when a fourteen-year-old student and son of private investigator, David Fournette, was rescued during a daring FBI raid. The boy, whose name will not be released because of his age, was allegedly held by a known drug dealer, Alonzo Chambers.

"Authorities speculate the drug dealer was motivated by revenge. Further complicating the investigation, Mr. Chambers was found dead in his New Orleans East residence. Police are still looking at leads, but believe his killing was motivated by a clash between competing drug rings.

"The parents of the rescued boy are neither commenting nor granting interviews at this time."

Alan Smith contacted David after the headlines broke and the news segments aired. David still wasn't comfortable with his name sprayed across the newspapers. For his family, privacy was hard to come by.

"Did you see it?" Smith asked.

"How could I miss it…right on the front page?"

Alan decided it was best to break the news.

"David, we've discussed how to proceed with our investigation of the Marascos."

"So, what's the plan?"

"Everything we've released for public consumption places blame for the kidnapping on Lonnie Chambers."

"Right, go on."

"We're thinking it's best to back off the intense assault on street drugs... go back to our normal enforcement."

"Don't take this the wrong way, Alan, but normal didn't work so well."

"Hear me through?"

"Okay, go."

"Right about now, Jim and Tony Marasco feel pretty good about themselves. The more secure they feel, the quicker they'll return to importing 25i."

"I dunno, Tony Marasco is not like his son," said David. "He's a devious but patient man. It's more likely he'll nix the drugs for awhile and rely on his legal businesses."

"We understand that, but he won't abandon the drug business forever, too much money involved. We intend to monitor every shipment. Eventually..."

"Eventually my ass! How long is that?"

"Listen, David, we gotta be smart about this."

"I guess Rick Donner could keep us informed." David tried his best to calm down.

"Exactly. As soon as we determine a shipment includes the Condimento, or any product gets delivered directly to Marasco's business location, we plan to go in."

David grunted affirmatively, but he did have concerns. Would Tony Marasco really become more careless due to the FBI's seeming disinterest? He doubted it. At the same time, Brenda had urged him to get back to his normal business routine, and leave the Marascos to the authorities. They had seen nothing but chaos and violence since Billy's death, and she felt it was time for them to let others worry about the Marasco family. She felt empathy for Tom and Nancy, but not to the tune of sacrificing her own children.

"I know you will keep me informed, Alan."

"Of course."

"I'll keep my ear close to the ground, but I won't do anything to spook them."

David decided to back off any direct confrontation for now, but he planned to watch the Marascos like a hawk.

Jim Marasco was feeling his oats. His behavior became even more bizarre than usual. His nights out on the town were more absurd, and the parties held at the Creole Cottage were out of control. He stayed away from David and his family, but a bitterness and rage with the Fournettes still consumed him.

In one week's time, Jim managed to further jeopardize his father's trust. In the early morning hours, a neighbor's noise complaint brought police to his Rue Orleans cottage. Though that was not all that unusual for a Jim Marasco party, what stood out was how he chose to deal with the situation.

One of Jim's people answered the doorbell and found a dispatched police officer.

"We would like to speak to the owner of the house. We've received a nuisance complaint about loud music."

Jim walked unsteadily to the door. A mixture of alcohol, energy drinks and an empty stomach reinforced his sour demeanor. He was in no mood to deal with the police.

"I'm Jim Marasco!" he shouted. "Who's the asshole that's complaining about the noise?"

The officer made an attempt to diffuse the situation.

"Mr. Marasco, that's not important."

"It is to me!" he slurred.

"What is important is," the officer said calmly over the loud music, "you're not in compliance with the noise ordinance. If you don't tone it down, we'll shut down the party and take you into custody."

Jim was irate. He lunged forward just as one of his men grabbed him from behind and shoved him back into the room.

"I'll handle it, Boss. Go back to the party."

"I'm tired of these assholes!" Jim yelled pulling away from another associate. "Don't they have anything better to do?"

The officers vowed to return if Jim failed to heed their warning. As the policemen pulled back, Jim walked out on his front balcony and yelled to any neighbor who could hear.

"If I find which of you bastards complained, somebody gonna be dead!"

Two days later, in a French Quarter bar, Jim Marasco had the audacity to accost a female patron while her boyfriend was ordering drinks. The woman brushed off his advances, but Jim persisted. The boyfriend made the mistake of challenging the aggressor, and two of Jim's men beat him badly. The bar owner made an attempt to call the police, but the couple begged him not to.

As he and his goons left the bar, the depraved Jim Marasco said, "I'll take my money elsewhere, if you don't want my business. And get this little bitch outta my sight!"

⚜

Tony Marasco had asked Gendusa to keep an eye on Jim, but he did not like the reports. He was angry with Jim, but deep down, he still felt an obligation to protect him. It was pride as much as fatherly love that motivated him to shield his wayward son at the expense of his own peril. The news of Jim's reckless behavior worried him even more, and he knew something had to give.

Tony watched the newsfeeds and read the newspaper with interest. It pleased him that Lonnie Chambers was fingered as the person behind the Fournette kidnapping. He was sure David Fournette knew better, but it was good to see that the Marasco name was never implicated. Trying to determine the future of his business, he discussed the current environment with Gendusa.

"John, what are you hearing on the street?"

"It's quiet." Gendusa was a man of few words.

"How do you mean, quiet?"

"The police are visible, but the word is, budget cuts are causing them to reduce enforcement."

"Just as I told you: good things come to those who wait."

"Yeah. There's a lot of grousing by the rank and file, you know, complaining they don't have the manpower."

"What about the feds...and Fournette?"

"That's quiet too."

"I need specifics." Tony wasn't interested in generalities.

"The feds disbanded the CARD team once the kid was found, and local agents have their hands full with a huge city corruption investigation. You know, the shit about bribing that Williams guy on the City Council. Too bad they don't know bribes flow like water."

"It seems we can always count on our political friends to take some of the heat," Tony chuckled. "But that won't stop Fournette."

"As for the P.I., we keep reasonably close tabs. Right now he is working a case for an insurance company dealing with the theft of some expensive paintings."

"Good, let him find another bone to chew on."

"It's like you said, Boss, he has to do something to feed his family. His wife probably suggested he do just that."

Tony eased back in his chair with a warm smile.

"I owe you a debt of gratitude, John. Your good work has helped us avert disaster."

"That's my job, Boss. I'll do what it takes to protect this family. However, there is some news that ain't so good."

Tony leaned forward. "Tell me."

"Jim can't seem to keep his nose out of trouble. He could bring more unwanted attention."

Tony fumed as Gendusa outlined the events of the last week. *My son is a disaster,* he thought rubbing his forehead. He paused for a few seconds and the room was silent. Finally, he looked up at Gendusa and spoke.

"I need to talk to Franco, you know, about our future plans. He'll want to know if we can receive our scheduled shipment."

"Yeah, I guess."

"He will grow impatient if our cash flow is further interrupted."

"What do we do about Jim?"

"He threatens our family. We gotta do something."

"Yes, we do."

"Perhaps I can discuss my troubled son with Franco. Maybe it's time for him to go."

CHAPTER 14

Franco Romano was working on a stainless steel fermentation tank in the winery. One of the valves had leaked causing him to lose juice that would have produced at least two barrels of finished product. He was in a shitty mood.

"Mama Mia, what willa happen next?" he said. "Angelo, getta over here and clean up this shit."

"Imma comin', Mr. Romano."

"Get that puttana, Maria, to help you!" he yelled. "Do I gotta do everything myself?"

Romano cursed his bad luck and the stainless steel tank. It was not the way he wanted to start his day. He hoped that was the end of his bad news. In the midst of all the chaos, he received an international call. It was from Tony Marasco. Tony's voice sounded almost cheerful.

"How are you, my brother?" Tony asked.

The still aggravated Romano sighed.

"I'm not worth a shit. It's not enough I have federal inspectors snooping around. Now I'm losing my wine because of a faulty valve."

"Not well, huh?"

"Dolce Gesu!" (Sweet Jesus!) Romano exclaimed into the phone.

"Hang in there," Tony chuckled supportively. "It will get better."

"It better happen soon, or I'll be out of business."

"I need to give you an update on what is happening in New Orleans."

"No more bad news, please!"

"Apparently, the polizia are running short of denaro," Tony crowed. "For the most part, the street is back to normal."

"Finally, something good. Has your inquisitive friend moved on to other ventures, as well?"

"It appears he has. He needs to get back to making some money. Like us, he has mouths to feed."

"Do you think it will stay that way?" Romano asked.

"Perhaps, though he is a persistent one."

"Hmmm?"

"I hope he has seen enough misfortune to stay away from us," Tony said.

"Ah! That news almost makes me forget about my wasted vino."

"See, I can bring good news."

"So, if they have lost interest, perhaps we can get back to business?"

"That is what I am thinking."

"It's about time. My manufacturing operation must earn its keep."

"Franco, I do have a favor to ask of you?"

"Here it comes. What would that be?'

"Things are not going well with Jim."

"Oh, your wayward son?"

"He can do many things right when he is thinking straight, but right now he is making some poor decisions…the kind that could cost us."

Romano had heard Jim could be a handful. Though he had limited personal experience, he knew his indiscretions had caused much of their current problems.

"What is causing this attitude?" Romano asked.

"I'm not sure, but I think he is pressing because he knows he has disappointed me."

Romano reflected for a second and spoke.

"Jim is not a man who will stand by when he thinks there is a problem. He has pride, but as we all know, pride can sometimes get you in trouble."

"That is right, my friend. At times he acts and then he thinks later."

"What can I do to help?" Romano was almost afraid to ask.

"I am wondering if Jim would benefit from seeing your end of the business."

"Have him come here?"

"Yes, it would help him understand our mutual interest…and remove him from the lifestyle that is hindering his judgment."

What little Romano knew of Jim, he didn't like. Bringing him under his roof did not sit well, but he knew he and Tony had obligations to each other. He was in a difficult position.

"You know I amma willing to help you in any way I can, but how willa Jim react to this news?"

"It depends."

"On what?"

"If he feels he is back in my good graces, and helping to get the business back on track…"

"In other words, make him feel he is, how do you say, important?"

"That's it! Besides, who wouldn't like to spend a few weeks in the beautiful Tuscan countryside?"

Romano could see this cup was not going to pass away from him. Refusal would be very disrespectful to his friend and business associate. He resolved to make the best of it.

"Then it is done. I willa make sure I involve him in the winery business. Perhaps he will learn how to fix a leaky valve?"

The two men laughed heartily.

"Franco, before I leave you, I need a few more momenti to discuss our next shipment."

Alan Smith was frustrated. He and his men were in "hurry up and then wait" mode. It was a touchy balance to stay closely abreast of Marasco shipments while making sure there were no leaks from the numerous confidants the power broker had under the cover of payroll.

Unfortunately, things were very normal at Marasco & Marasco. FBI surveillance of the Tchoupitoulas office and warehouse was not very productive. From what they could gather, the Marascos seemed engaged only with their legal business ventures. The next shipment into the Port of New Orleans was due in a week. Smith was reasonably sure they would get advance information on the contents of the shipment, as well as the ultimate product destination.

Smith was catching his own share of heat since FBI resources were stretched thin, and presently the political corruption trial going on in the city garnered much of the attention of the decision makers.

Smith met David for lunch to catch up on things.

"Any momentum on the Marasco investigation?" David asked.

"The brass and big shots are not that interested, now. But just you wait. If we blow the lid off of this case, destabilize the illegal drug trade, and solve a few murders, they will all climb out of the woodwork to take credit."

"Those guys do love their fifteen minutes of fame," David snickered. "Me, I just want to put the Marascos behind bars."

"I'm with you on that."

"Sure does gall me," David said. "Saw a society page picture of Tony and his wife at a big charity fundraiser."

"Gotta keep up appearances."

"Guy should be behind bars. Instead, he's being praised for his good works."

"I'll keep you posted when I have clearance to proceed."

Smith knew they would need to cover their bases on this one. He wondered if they would be best served intercepting the shipment while it still sat on the docks at the Louisiana Terminal. That was an option, but one thing bothered him. What if they found the drugs before Marasco took physical possession? Would Tony claim he had no knowledge of the contents and place blame on Bella Ballerina? It was possible.

There is no honor among thieves, Smith thought, *when someone's about to take a fall.*

Perhaps he was over thinking this, but just in case, his first option was to follow the goods until they were under Marasco's control, and then strike.

Smith was asked to share his plan with the Special Agent in Charge, Andy Hammond. A screw up here had the potential to embarrass the agency, which was never a good thing.

"It appears we have a 'go' when the shipment arrives next week," Smith explained.

His boss arched his eyebrows as one might when he hears something with the potential to be very good or very bad.

"Alan, you have a 'go,' when I say you have a 'go'. I'm the Agent in Charge, you know, the one whose ass is on the line. Do I make myself clear?"

"I... uh... didn't mean to come across..."

"Are all aspects of this sting operation double-checked? Any loopholes?"

"We've gone over it a hundred times. We think our plan is sound."

"Go over it again! This is very sensitive. Failure will undermine our operations in this district for a long time, not to mention my own position."

"Andy, we won't fail. We've given the target every reason to believe we've backed off and are out of the picture. I believe we are well positioned."

"And what if it's not there?"

"It'll be there. Trust me."

Hammond nodded, but his words were not very supportive.

"It better be, Alan. I'm counting on you. Don't betray my trust."

Smith remembered his numerous conversations with David. He hoped the new plan would pay dividends. David had doubts, but had reluctantly agreed to let the FBI bring down the Marascos. Smith had convinced him he had done his part while creating substantial risk to his family. He did not want to let his friend down. At this point, all that was left to do was wait…wait…wait. The one week wait would seem like an eternity.

⚜

Jim could hardly believe it. Tony had invited him to dinner at the family's Audubon residence. *The old guy's getting soft,* he thought. When the doorbell rang, an attractive middle-aged woman, thin with well coiffed blond hair, rushed to the leaded, bevel-glass front doors to greet her son.

From Jim's point of view Angela was an ideal wife. She had the class and good looks to accompany his father to any society function while affording him the deference and respect he felt he deserved and expected. Best of all, she didn't ask questions or want to know about Tony's business. Tony had told him that years ago she had attempted small-talk when she saw Tony acknowledge an unsavory looking character as they walked from a downtown restaurant. Tony simply said, "He is not a man you need to know." *She likes the good life,* Jim thought.

"Jim, I'm so glad to see you!" Angela gushed. "Hattie has prepared a wonderful dinner for you."

"For me? That's great, Momma," he answered.

"You look thin, Jim. Are you eating well? You need some home cooking."

"I'm fine, why do you always worry?"

Hattie had been their long time employee, and for the most part she had had the lead role of feeding and clothing Jim from as far back as he could remember.

Dinner was casual and uneventful. Hattie served a great meal of Trout Meuniere, and Tony uncorked a fine bottle of Caymus Cabernet. Angela talked incessantly and had tons of questions, but Jim did not mind. It pleased him that his mother was so overjoyed to have dinner with her son. He was always happy when people doted on him, and this was no exception.

After dinner, Tony lit a cigar. He looked serious.

"Angela, Jim and I will have an after-dinner drink in my study and discuss some business. Will you excuse us?"

"Certainly," she dutifully answered. "I'll check on Hattie and see her out." She leaned down. "Love you, Jim. I'm so glad you came for dinner."

Tony led his son into the study and closed the Mahogany French doors behind them. Father and son settled into two deep-brown, leather club chairs. The fireplace in the opulent study danced softly providing a warm glow. Tony poured a glass of Drambuie for him and his son.

"Jim, I am in need of your services."

"You need me?"

"I feel the climate is somewhat better now, don't you think?"

"Yeah, it looks like the dick and his cop friends got the message." He wanted to say, *I told you so!*

"I need you to spend some time with Franco Romano."

"Italy? What good can I do there?" Jim asked.

"We are at a very critical point in our relationship. I would feel better if you were there to protect our family's interest as Romano prepares the next few Bella Ballerina shipments."

"Make sure he's doing right by us?"

"I trust Franco, but sending you will show our commitment to a long term relationship."

"If that's what you want, I'll do it." Jim wondered what his father was up to, but he loved those Italian women.

"I'm not getting any younger, Jim. One day…"

"Yeah, sure, it'll all be mine," Jim laughed.

"We have a lot at stake. I want you to have a strong relationship with this key friend and partner."

Jim reflected on his father's comments. Things had not been good between the two of them, but his intentions seemed genuine. Tony would not even trust Gendusa with this assignment. He thought, *Blood is thicker than water*.

"That's fine, Dad. I would like to learn more about Franco's manufacturing operation. You know I'll make sure I protect our interest."

"Good, good, my son."

"When do you want me to leave for Italy?"

"Right away. I need you to supervise the next shipment."

"I'll make the arrangements."

Tony stood and embraced his son.

"Jim, I know the last number of weeks have been tough, but here is a chance for us to move forward together. There are brighter days ahead."

Jim felt...important.

Chapter 15

It was a lovely summer morning when Jim Marasco's short flight from Rome landed in Florence. The temperature was a pleasant 75 degrees Fahrenheit, well below the expected high of 87. Franco Romano had dispatched a limo to pick up his honored guest at *Aeroporto di Firenze-Peretola*. The uniformed driver walked Jim to the car, opened the rear door and leaned in to uncover an iced compartment between the seats.

"Welcome...a welcome to Italy. Mr. Romano welcomes you."

"Thank you." Jim rubbed his eyes still suffering from jet lag.

"May I offer you a juice, chilled water or Bella Ballerina Chianti?"

Jim shrugged then held up his hand. He plopped into the overstuffed, leather seat.

"Sit a back and enjoy the scenery. Only a 81 kilometers to Cortona."

As they rode south, Jim felt good about his visit. He took off his sports coat and sat back to take in the sights. The rolling hills created a backdrop to the beautifully symmetrical rows of grapevines and olive trees. He felt relaxed.

They entered a single lane roadway, and Jim depressed the window button to better experience the sights, sounds and smells of the countryside. The air carried whiffs of Lavender, Rosemary and ornamental flowers. The driver pointed out the ancient Etruscan tombs. It was easy to see why his old man loved the area so much. Jim smiled and thought, *I could get used to this.*

The limo pulled up to a large gravel road bordered by vineyards and a lush olive grove. Jim admired the beautiful stone and wood-beamed winery and lush, fragrant gardens. Then the vision of Romano's limestone villa appeared on the horizon, and he thought again, *I could really get used to this.*

As the limo passed a beautiful, old, stone fountain, Jim saw the couple walk off the portico. Though he had met Franco Romano only a few times, he instantly recognized the diminutive man in the white, silk shirt and camel corduroy vest. As he exited the vehicle, Romano shook his hand.

Damn, is this the old man's wife? he wondered. *What a looker!*

"It is nice to see you again, Jim," Romano said. "Welcome to our home."

"Happy to be here."

"I don't believe you've met my wife, Bella."

Jim tried not to stare and extended his hand to the striking woman. The ever friendly and very Italian Bella instead pulled him in close and bestowed a typical Italian greeting, a kiss on each cheek.

"We are happy for your visit," the beautiful woman gushed.

"It is good to meet you," Jim said, smelling her perfume. *Very good. This babe has it all.*

It was impossible to overlook Bella's sleek lines, her dark-blue riding tights, and coffee-colored boots framed long dancer legs and a perfectly proportioned backside. *How did he land this? The old fart's my hero already.*

"Let's get you settled in," Bella said, "and then we will have some lunch."

"Sounds good to me."

"After, I will show you around the property," Romano said, "and we can discuss business."

"Excellent."

"As you know there is an important shipment for your father that will leave here tomorrow."

After putting his things away, Jim walked down the stone staircase to meet his host for lunch. He hoped Bella would join them. He had a hard time getting the image of the beautiful, olive-skinned dancer with long, silky black hair out of his head.

Alan Smith worked closely with David's friend, Rick Donner, at the Port of New Orleans. He was given word that the next Bella Ballerina shipment from the Port of Genoa would arrive in approximately six days. As best they could determine, the shipment would contain the usual products and quantities, including the Condimento Balsamica which historically was picked up by Marasco employees and moved directly to their Tchoupitoulas location nearby.

Smith was elated with the plan when he called his friend.

"David, it looks like the Marascos took the bait."

"Yeah, Donner's info seems to support that."

"I can smell it. We've got his ass!"

"Don't count your chickens."

"But…"

"The old man's sly, Alan. I wonder if I could get a look at the stuff as soon as it's offloaded?"

"How would you do that?"

"Maybe a stevedore drops a crate?" David said.

"No good. For an airtight case, the drugs need to be in Marasco's possession."

"I don't like it. The longer we wait the more time for something to go wrong."

"Don't screw it up, David. We will track the shipment from its Genoa origin to New Orleans. When the Condimento arrives at the Louisiana Avenue wharf, it will be constantly monitored."

"But what if…"

"If and when the drugs are moved to Marasco's facility, we will be armed with the appropriate warrants to inspect the product containing the 25i."

"I suppose you're right. But it's risky."

"This is a risky business."

August 1st, 2012 was a rainy day in New Orleans. It was no light mist but the type of gully-washer that appeared suddenly and with enough vengeance to cause local flooding. Smith thought, *Bad omen. Can't offload the merchandize in this. Seems even Mother Nature is on the side of the Marascos.*

David agreed to watch the FBI operation from a surveillance vehicle. The Special Agent in Charge felt he should not be directly involved in the actual execution of the sting.

After much delay, suddenly, it was game on.

In the early afternoon under a steady downpour, stevedores removed the Marasco shipment from the cargo ship and placed it at the entrance of the temperature-controlled facility. Surveillance teams closely observed the process and quickly deduced the suspected drug product was being segregated from the remainder of the shipment, as it was being moved into the Louisiana Avenue Terminal.

Smith immediately suspected something was up. Within minutes, a white Ford transit van entered the terminal and pulled up directly into the dock's pickup area. A driver and occupant exited the van and walked toward the dock superintendent.

Smith switched on his live electronic communication. "Target vehicle is a white Ford van. Trigger should be positioned with visual of the terminal gate. When the van exits, trigger will handoff to layup to execute the follow."

The FBI utilized a floating box technique to maintain contact with a target vehicle. Trigger vehicles typically watched as the vehicle began moving, and then would handoff to more nondescript vehicles for the pursuit.

In moments the two occupants of the white van flashed identification and port documents authorizing them to load the ten isolated cases of merchandise. There was no attempt to restrict the movement of the targeted goods. Smith instead, wanted the Marasco's to take direct possession. The target vehicle exited the terminal and then turned right on Tchoupitoulas Street toward downtown.

Smith quickly communicated, "Target vehicle headed away from the Marasco facility. Follow vehicles maintain visual."

"Roger."

Smith radioed David.

"That's odd. Must be headed to a different drop point."

"A wild goose chase," David replied.

"Don't lose 'em," Smith commanded.

The van led them through much of the downtown area, turning onto Canal Street and heading away from the river. Follow vehicles handed off to avoid suspicion. After twenty minutes of random driving, the van did a "U" turn and seemed to be heading back to the Louisiana Avenue Terminal.

"Christ!" Smith swore. "They're onto us. No…no wait."

The van passed the terminal, stopped at the Marasco & Marasco gate and entered the facility.

Smith smiled. *Got 'em!*

"What a sorry excuse of misdirection," Smith reported. "An FBI academy rookie could have maintained that tail."

"Almost, too easy," David replied.

Smith instructed his team to stop any vehicle entering or leaving the Marasco office and warehouse.

"Damn, I feel helpless," David said. "Wish I could go in."

"Just hang tight, brother."

Smith was accompanied by a chemist from the FBI's Chemical and Forensic Unit. He would examine the product on site.

Three Bureau units pulled up to the import facility. Smith walked confidently toward the guard and handed him a warrant giving the team authority to search the premises and examine any contents.

"FBI!" Smith announced. "We have a warrant."

"Wait here, I'll get my boss."

"Yeah, sure, we're goin' in."

"But you can't…"

"Watch me!"

Smith charged ahead with five men as the gate guard picked up the phone. Two members of the FBI team remained at the gate while three agents stood guard at the front of the warehouse.

Smith and two of his people with guns drawn confronted Tony Marasco and John Gendusa at the doorway of his office. Both men had a scowl on their faces. If looks could kill, Alan Smith would have been a dead man.

Tony stood rigidly and sneered. "What is the meaning of this? Why do you burst into my business waving guns and making threats?"

"Mr. Marasco, I'm Assistant Special Agent Alan Smith. We have warrants to search the entire property including your warehouse and the shipment you just received."

"And what? Is it now illegal to ship balsamic and wine into the country?"

"No, but…"

"I have all my licenses and shipping documents…you would like to review them?"

"That won't be necessary. What we do need is for you to open the locking system to the warehouse, so we can examine your shipment."

"I'd like to see that warrant." Tony scanned it and shook his head softly.

"Open up."

"You are making a big mistake. John, let us walk downstairs, so Assistant Special Agent Smith will see the folly of his ways."

Gendusa walked to the door of the warehouse and placed his print against the keypad. The lock on the large door immediately snapped open. The agents poured into the facility while Gendusa and Tony Marasco stood silently just inside the entrance to the warehouse.

Smith instructed an agent to pry open one of the balsamic crates. He then looked to the chemist.

"Mr. Kim, would you do us the honor of analyzing the contents of these bottles?"

Kim set his field kit up on a table, and took the lid off a bottle from the opened crate. The chemist had an immediate reaction when the odor floated to his nostrils.

"My God! This stuff stinks."

He looked quizzically at Smith, but continued with a quick chemical analysis. In a matter of five minutes, he looked up and made his pronouncement.

"This is undoubtedly…balsamic vinegar."

"What did you jackasses expect?" Tony Marasco chided.

The words cut through to Smith's midsection like a knife. He immediately felt a mixture of embarrassment and fear course through his body.

"Open up another box!" he ordered.

The confused team complied, and after a few agonizing minutes, Mr. Kim delivered the same verdict.

"Balsamic vinegar."

Smith looked around the room in a panic, but there was no more product to test. He turned to face Tony Marasco who suppressed a wicked smile and then responded slowly, yet sternly.

"Agent Smith, I warned you. I am not going to stand for this slander to my good name. The FBI will be hearing from my lawyer. You have jeopardized your career by harassing an honest businessman."

Smith responded almost sheepishly, "Marasco, I've underestimated your guile."

"Whatever do you mean, guile? And by the way, that's Mr. Marasco to you."

Smith instructed his men to withdraw immediately from the property. As he departed he walked the short distance to David's waiting car.

"We're fucked!" It was all he could think to say.

"I heard," said David. "It really sucks."

"The bastards must've been tipped off," Smith whined.

"Or…maybe they just outsmarted us."

"Yeah, maybe."

"Marasco didn't get this far by being stupid," David stated the obvious. "How many people knew about this operation."

"Quite a few."

"Well…there's your answer."

"I'm gonna pay big time for this," Smith sighed.

"And it'll take an Act of Congress to go after Marasco now."

"Tell me about it."

"Brenda made me promise to stay out of it, but under the circumstances…"

"David, what could you do?"

" Pray?" David said with a blank stare. "Dear Lord, give me some Divine Inspiration."

CHAPTER 16

❧

Jim Marasco and Franco Romano sat enthralled as they listened to Tony on the speakerphone in Romano's office. Jim beamed with pride. Finally his father had come up with some good ideas.

"You shudda seen his face, when the chemist told him it was balsamica. I thought he was gonna have a heart attack and drop right there."

"Our plan worked to perfection," said Jim.

"You made 'em look like…what's that show…yeah, *The Three Stooges*," Romano said.

All three men laughed heartily, enthused and pleased with their fiendish ingenuity. Tony had convinced his Italian partner and his son to do this dry run. Something in his makeup caused him to sense a threat, and move to counter it. Of course, Tony had noticed the feds staking out his home and the docks. He knew what to expect, because he had seen it all before.

It wasn't too difficult to convince Romano to go along, when Tony told him he would pay just as if the shipment contained the 25i. His friend maintained his cash flow, and Tony avoided a well conceived FBI threat.

A small price to pay, Jim thought, *to screw the feds.*

Romano chuckled. "You my friend are, as they say, one for the ages. Can you imagine the ball busting going on at the FBI headquarters?"

"We are getting word," Tony replied, "that Alan Smith and the Special Agent in Charge have both received reprimands."

"Keep the bastardos on the run."

"Don't worry, I've filed a suit…harassment, slander, damage to property. They will be occupied for awhile."

Jim flashed the same vile emotion he had become known for.

"Good for the bastards," he said. "What do they say, if you mess with the bee, you will get stung? What will be our next move?"

Tony responded with the exuberance of a man that had just won the lottery.

"Tonight we celebrate! Tomorrow we set our new plan in motion."

"We have much to celebrate," Romano said. "Time to enjoy a good meal."

"Jim, make sure you take Franco and Bella to my favorite restaurant, Cibo e Amicizia. Food and friendship, it doesn't get any better than that. Oh! And Jim, make sure you send me the bill."

There was a lighthearted mood at Romano's villa. Jim looked forward to a night on the town, and it did not hurt that the sexy Bella would be joining them. He shaved, showered and gelled his slick-backed hair. Almost as an afterthought, he splashed on some of the aftershave from an ornate bottle on the bathroom vanity. It had a rich, woody smell that he liked, not like those sweet, perfumery ones he hated.

He looked in the mirror one final time and admired the black, cashmere tee nestled under his dark grey Gabardine sports coat. Jim had a high opinion of his appearance, and looking smart was an important feature of his persona.

Time to hit town with that good looking broad, he thought. Bella was fast becoming an obsession.

As they waited for Bella, Romano and Jim sat enjoying a glass of his best Chianti. Romano's back was to the door when Bella entered the villa's spacious living room. Jim looked up while avoiding Romano's gaze. It seemed he almost had to catch his breath.

The statuesque beauty moved toward them. She wore a short, black dress and black, satin stiletto heels. Bella moved seductively. There was a spring in her step, with one foot alternating directly in front of the other generating a swivel in her well contoured hips.

"Are my two handsome escorts ready for a nice dinner and night on the town?" Bella asked.

"You look wonderful, my dear. What do you think, Jim?" Romano inquired.

"Absolutely, I'm honored to be one of your escorts, Bella."

"We are off for a night of good vino and great food," Romano said exuberantly.

Romano was well known to the owner of Cibo e Amicizia and its restaurant personnel. As soon as he and Bella entered the restaurant, the owner, Luigi, shuffled over to greet them. His short, stout frame seemed to complement a receding hairline and a few random, grey curls protruding from the crown of his head. The gregarious Italian opened his arms and hugged them warmly.

In Italian he exclaimed, "How honored I am to see my wonderful friends."

"Luigi, this is my American friend, Jim Marasco," Romano said in English. "You have met his papa, Tony, many times."

"I do remember him," the affable and portly Italian responded with exaggerated flare. "He is a fine man, your father. If I remember right, Franco, he loves my homemade egg noodles."

Romano chuckled.

"You do have a good memory, my old friend."

"Sit, sit, we fill up your stomachs. Let me tell Dario you are here."

Luigi always had Dario wait on Romano's table. Bella liked him, and he made the Romanos feel as though he was there only to serve them. They always got the small, round table near the fountain that graced the middle of the festive and ornate restaurant. Even if customers were already there, they were simply shooed away. The trickling water had a calming effect and added a romantic flare.

Jim couldn't take his eyes off Bella, but his meal of *Bistecca alla fiorentina* and Italian pasta was delicious.

"This food is fit for a king," he exclaimed.

"Yes," Romano laughed, "it tastes even better when you are paying."

A sober Jim could exude charm; his good looks and athletic frame helped him stand out in a crowd. Unfortunately, that charismatic and friendly disposition tended to diminish in direct proportion to the amount of alcohol consumed. He was a mean drunk. Whatever inhibitions the mercurial Jim Marasco possessed also tended to diminish as the number of drinks increased.

Bella Romano sat between her husband and Jim. Throughout the evening, she had exchanged furtive glances with the handsome young American. Even when she was not looking at him, Jim could sense the warmth of her passion. The forty-five-year-old woman seemed delighted in knowing a man over ten years her junior could be consumed by her seductive powers.

Bella wants me, Jim thought.

As they awaited their dessert of roasted peaches with Amaretti, the slightly tipsy Romano announced he was headed to the toilette. Jim watched as he stopped to engage Luigi in small talk and then headed to the restroom. Jim leaned a little closer to Bella. His leg touched hers as he put his right hand at the top of her chair.

"Bella, I'm very happy you could join us tonight. I hope it does not offend you when I say you are a beautiful and sensuous woman."

The flirtatious beauty casually tossed her raven hair and turned her head slightly toward him. Her smile and curious eyes failed to reveal any defined emotion.

"You make me blush, but I am pleased to hear such a young and handsome man tell me this."

That was all Jim needed. Adroitly, he moved his left hand under the black tablecloth toward Bella's leg. She sighed. Encouraged, he slowly moved his hand up Bella's inner thigh. She gasped slightly while maintaining a serene smile. Her hand moved to simply cover his, only stopping its progress, but not removing it.

"Jim, though your touch arouses me, I fear my husband might look at it much differently. We would not want an awkward moment or tension in your business relationship, would we?"

"Does he need to know?"

Bella said "back off" with her eyes.

"Perhaps, another day... another time." With that she squeezed Jim's hand and placed it back on the table.

As Romano returned from behind them, Jim wondered, *Oh shit, what did he see?* He shifted in his seat away from Bella. *Ah, the petty jealousy of an older man with a beautiful wife,* he thought. *Guess I should be ashamed of myself.*

The three enjoyed dessert and an after-dinner drink. There was no discernible difference in anyone's mood or demeanor. For some reason Romano suddenly seemed uneasy. Jim felt daggers. He wanted to make a move on Bella, but he only had one more week to do it.

"You guys wanna head to the bar?" Jim asked.

"I believe we had better head back to the villa," Romano said with a cold tone. "We have a busy day tomorrow, and we will also have another call with your father to discuss our upcoming plans."

"Whatever, Franco, I can hang with the best of them, but I understand."

Jim inhaled her perfume and pictured Bella sprawled over a big double bed. The ride home was quiet, but he could feel her lustful magnetism. He didn't care about the risk, he only wanted to trap her in a hallway or broom closet. His mind reeled with the possibilities.

CHAPTER 17

David checked on his friend, Alan Smith. He knew he was feeling the heat, and he hoped this latest setback would not completely squash FBI support of the Marasco investigation. The switch Tony pulled had given Special Agent in Charge, Andy Hammond, a massive black eye, and he was not a happy camper. Smith was lucky he still had his job.

"Alan, I've been thinking about you," David said. "Are things settling down?"

"No chance!" Smith replied. "The shit's really hit the fan."

"What's the latest?"

"If you can believe it, my boss actually received a call from the Director."

"No shit?"

"It was not a call of congratulations."

"The Director of the FBI...called Andy Hammond?"

"Yeah, can you believe it? My screw up caused Hammond to get a dressing down from the Director of the fucking FBI? As you can guess, I'm pretty high up on his shit list."

"It may be tough now, but we all know the Marascos are as dirty as they come."

"Dirty, but slippery," Smith said. "I found out the hard way."

"They won't cease their drug business, it's too lucrative. They'll be back."

"Question is, will I be here to help stop them?"

"The Marascos threw us a curve, Alan. If the FBI washes their hands of this, they will be faced with an even larger publicity debacle when more people die."

"That may be the case," Smith groaned, "but right now they have me in mothballs."

"Are you completely shut down?"

"I'm not saying I won't be able to help at some point, but basically, you'll need to carry the ball now. We need some concrete information that will bring down these thugs."

That wasn't the answer David had hoped for. He understood, like it or not, he was being thrust back into the forefront in this quest to stop the Maracos. So far, the local FBI district had only lost some self respect, but any additional screw up would mean demotion or loss of jobs.

Brenda and David sat at the kitchen table. They were alone. The boys had friends over for pizza and video games, and David could hear the din of the Major League Baseball video in the background. It sounded like there was a war going on.

"Quiet!" Brenda shouted to no avail.

"Do teenagers ever do anything quietly?" David said with mock disdain.

"Hardly. You should know, sometimes you still act like a big kid."

"Got to admit, you're right about that."

David pushed the food around on his dinner plate, not saying much.

"How is work going?" Brenda asked raising one eyebrow.

"Pretty well, I was able to recover the paintings for the insurance company."

"Good job, hon. Your client must be happy."

"Would you care to guess who stole them?"

"Inside job?"

"My wife solves the crime in a split second, and I'm supposed to be the detective?" He laughed.

"Call it intuition."

"You're right, Bren. The owner built up some very large debt. He was living large, as they say. Collecting a quarter-million in insurance money would have been just what the doctor ordered."

"Too bad for him, David Fournette was on the case."

"Guy will spend most of what he has left defending against felony fraud charges."

"That's what he gets for being a crook, and messin' with my man."

Brenda walked behind David's chair and massaged his neck.

"Oooo, that feels…"

"If things are going well, why are you so tense? Your muscles are as tight as guitar strings."

"Alan is taking a beating over this failed FBI raid."

"I suspected as much."

"Obviously, I feel bad for him, but the Special Agent in Charge also had his wrist slapped, and he's not that anxious to continue investigating you-know-who."

"These people are not only running a drug syndicate," she said, "they are ruthless killers. It's the FBI's responsibility to stay on this."

"Maybe so, but they feel they're backed into a corner."

Brenda sat back down and eyed David closely. He could feel her searching through his thoughts.

"There you go," she said, "slight frown…arched brow. You're not telling me something."

He turned away from her probing eyes.

"David Fournette! You're thinking of getting involved again?"

He thought twice about being honest with her. "Brenda, if I don't keep digging, these guys will skate, and more families will suffer."

Brenda showed her frustration, but understood David's predicament. She leaned down and caressed his neck.

"Please be careful, honey. I know you need to do what you believe is right, but we can't put the lives of our sons in jeopardy."

"They'll never get their dirty hands on my family again. I promise…on my life."

Jim Marasco still had a slight hangover when he sat down with Franco Romano to place an afternoon call to Tony. Although his head throbbed, Bella still lingered on his mind.

Romano eyed him suspiciously as he placed the call.

"What?" Jim said.

"Feeling homesick yet?" Romano mocked.

Before Jim could reply, his father picked up the phone.

Both men were happy to hear Tony say their next shipment would be the real deal; it would contain the synthetic drugs that their distributors were clamoring for.

More time to spend with Bella, Jim thought.

"We have played the cat and mouse game," Tony said, "and we ended up as the cat. Now we reap the benefits."

"Yes, yes." Romano nodded toward the phone. "We have ample supply; it will be no trouble meeting the demand."

"I would like to discuss a change…to our process," Tony offered.

Both men remained silent waiting for Tony to expand on his thoughts.

"The feds…they still have eyes on my Tchoupitoulas warehouse," Tony said. "We gave them a good punch in the nose, but they're still watching. Regardless, it is time to get the operation moving again."

"Money to be made," Romano said.

"Tell me about it," Tony said. "Last year we cleared four million on 25i alone...more than all my legitimate businesses."

"What change do you have in mind?" Jim asked.

"I've invested in some property," Tony declared. "There is a nice warehouse near Hammond just off I-10 and I-55. It is strategically located between New Orleans and our growing customer base in Baton Rouge."

"So we move it there instead?" Romano inquired.

"It is just what I was looking for. It's tucked away from prying eyes and has very good security."

The less perceptive, but still scheming Jim Marasco recognized where his father was going with this.

"So, we are taking our repackaging and distribution to a new location?"

"You're a genius," Tony mocked. "Maintaining this operation so close to home has many drawbacks. The authorities will be watching our people closely, and picking up the shipment from the Louisiana Avenue Wharf is still dangerous."

"What are your intentions, my friend?" asked the quizzical Romano.

"The warehouse was purchased in the name of a new corporation, T & J Distributing. That would be the abbreviation of my name and Jim's, but only we will know the connection."

"A new distribution point, huh?" Jim chimed in as though he wasn't paying attention.

"I just..." Tony sighed. "When the next shipment of Balsamica arrives, it will be shipped to distribution points just like the legitimate product. We will not touch it until it is repackaged for public distribution."

The always energetic Romano broke in.

"Great. There is nothing that will call attention to the 25i. It will be handled just like everything else."

"That's the plan."

"I think you've thought of everything. Jim and I will make sure everything goes well from our end."

"I'm counting on that; I know I can rely on you."

At the end of the call Tony mentioned that John Gendusa would be in charge at the warehouse from the time the goods arrived, during repacking, and until they left the new facility. He did not want anything left to chance. Gendusa would be onsite in case anything did go wrong.

The sound of Gendusa's name was enough to provoke Jim's ire. Recently, he had sensed an increased scorn from his father's trusted advisor. Though neither man spoke of it directly, they did not like or trust each other.

Gendusa! Jim swore to himself. *That asshole has my old man snowed.*

At the same time, when the chips were down, Jim knew Gendusa had the blend of physical and cognitive skills that made him a valuable ally and a feared adversary. Because of that, Jim did not register any concerns with Tony.

I guess, it all makes sense, he thought.

Besides, today he would be introduced to the man who actually manufactured the 25i. He was anxious to build a direct relationship with him. He had heard his father talk of the Albanian. Tony told him he was a mysterious character, maybe even a little off–the–wall, but a magician when it came to manufacturing drugs.

Never know, Jim thought, *if at some point my old man's out of the picture, Romano may outlive his usefulness.* The ever-selfish Jim Marasco always looked for a way to cut overhead and put more money in his pockets.

⚜

David had racked his brain and utilized every resource available to continue his investigation while maintaining his vow to Brenda. He had promised he would not directly challenge them, at least until he was sure he had the goods to put them away for a long time.

So far, David was unsuccessful placing an electronic listening device in Marasco's office. A systems engineer and friend had approached Marasco & Marasco about upgrading their commercial wireless network, but he was told in no uncertain terms, "We have all the systems expertise we need." That also limited David's opportunities to hack into their computer software.

David had enlisted the assistance of his old friend, Mark Harris, in his surveillance efforts. Harris would help whenever he was off duty or could poach some time from his police investigative duties. It took significant resources to monitor the property, vehicles, and people involved. David and Harris touched base at least once a day.

"Have you come across anything?" David asked.

"Hell no! You would think Tony and his man, Gendusa, were Altar Boys."

"Playing it straight, huh?"

"So it appears. Hey, what gives with Asshole Jim?"

"Tony sent him out of the country. Apparently, he's sequestered away at Franco Romano's estate in Italy."

"Another smart move...probably wanted that loose cannon out of the way."

"Sooner or later, they'll let their guard down."

David firmly believed every crook would make a mistake sooner or later. However, these were men who understood the need for surveillance recognition. David and Harris were always on alert, and great care and precautions were taken to avoid blowing their cover. David also knew, if they sighted him, they would hit back in any way possible. That was not something Brenda could further endure.

There were some close calls. David had followed John Gendusa and two of his cronies to an oyster house in the Lakeshore area, not too far from the New Orleans Yacht Club. He sat near the edge of the restaurant parking lot as the men ate. The three men exited around 9:00 p.m. The grey Buick sedan backed out onto Lakeshore Drive as if it were going to head south.

David had eased the Camaro SS into traffic about fifty yards behind the sedan. Just as abruptly as it had backed up, the vehicle pulled forward into the same parking space it had vacated. The move caused David to make a sharp left turn to avoid passing within feet of the men.

Damn, I've been made, he thought. He pulled over and watched in his rearview mirror.

Gendusa exited the vehicle, looked around suspiciously, and walked to the curb. He was on high alert, looking up and down the street before reentering the vehicle. David parked behind a large SUV, and the crew drove slowly by but failed to see the Camaro.

Surveillance seemed useless. There was no recognizable link to illegal activities; the comings and goings of the thugs mirrored those of legitimate businessmen.

David used his computer to research all of Marasco's public business records, but so far, they all dealt with Marasco's legitimate import business. Just when it looked like he was destined to wait and track the next Marasco shipment, David caught a break.

When Gendusa traveled alone, he drove a black Cadillac Escalade. The vehicle was always parked in the Marasco compound or inside the gate of Gendusa's uptown residence. During one of David's tails, Gendusa stopped at a convenience store. He parked the Escalade almost directly in front of the entrance. David parked his vehicle along the side of the building and walked as inconspicuously as possible toward the front. As luck would have it, Gendusa stood third in line waiting to check out with the convenience store clerk.

Moving quickly and covertly across the parking area, David leaned over as if to tie his shoe. It took only seconds to place a GPS locator under the right rear panel of the Escalade. He then walked back toward his car and away from the convenience store entrance. Within seconds, the unsuspecting Gendusa returned to his car.

David chuckled and thought, *Anyone with $300 and a laptop can track a target like the CIA. Guess that's okay if you're the one dong the tracking.*

CHAPTER 18

❦

Jim Marasco listened attentively as Armand Murati proudly explained the process of making 25i. The Albanian immigrated to Italy from Albania over a decade earlier. His country had seen much upheaval as it moved from socialism to democracy. For awhile after the revolution, the communists still controlled much of the government, but economic collapse caused further purging and an all out armed rebellion.

Murati had traveled the very short distance to Italy, not to escape corruption, but because of the massive crackdown on it. He had found numerous ways to traverse the economic and political uncertainty in Albania; cleaning it up was not to his benefit. He was a man whose skills seemed most suitable to illegal ventures.

"This guy knows his stuff, Franco," Jim said.

"Armand is a man of much talent. It all starts with him," Romano replied.

"You are very kind," the Albanian answered with artificial humility.

As Murati continued with his lesson, Romano received a phone call. It was apparent to Jim that the news was not good.

"What?" Jim asked as Romano turned off his cell.

"A representative of the Italian Ministry of Agriculture…he has appeared at my winery office unannounced."

"So?"

"He desires an inspection of the premises."

These unwanted interruptions had slowly decreased as FBI pressure on the Italian Federal Police or Guardia di Finanza diminished. The FBI could hardly push a foreign government when their own nose had been bloodied by the Marasco-fiasco. Old habits die hard, however, and the local inspectors continued to darken Romano's door, as much for job security as anything else.

"Inspection?"

"Gentleman, I must go. I had best do the walk through with the agricultural inspector myself."

"Don't these guys ever give up?" Jim shook his head in frustration. "Maybe you need to call his boss and allege harassment."

"What I don't need is more attention to my business."

"Keep him away from here." Murati looked worried.

"No problem, these buffone have a tendency to ease off, if you watch them closely. A case of vino as a small token of appreciation for their effort never hurts."

"Never pass up a good bribe," Jim chuckled with sarcasm. "I see they work here just like in the States."

"Bribe? No, no, my son, we don't use that word in Italy. I simply share some of my bounty with a poor government worker."

Jim wasn't unhappy that Romano had been called away. Without Romano hovering over him, he could talk openly with Murati. It was time to do some bonding.

"Armand, you are a valuable partner."

"Thank you for saying so, Mr. Marasco."

"The quality of your product is very critical to our business."

"This is nice to hear."

Jim pressed the issue, "I'm hopeful Mr. Romano treats you fairly and gives you the respect you deserve."

Murati did not immediately respond. He looked as though he was afraid to answer.

"It is my belief," Murati said, "that every man thinks he is worth more than what he is paid."

"Do you feel that way?"

Murati shrugged his shoulders. "I…I am happy…I have reasonable security in uncertain times."

"Obviously, this is just between us, but you should let me know if your arrangement with Franco causes you concern."

"Uh… but what would that accomplish? I am sure Mr. Romano would not appreciate such a conversation."

"He don't need to know," Jim answered. "That's why I'm talking to you in private. Who knows, we might both make more without a middleman."

Murati turned white as a sheet. "Oh…I must tell you I am very loyal to my friend, Mr. Romano. I would never…"

"Just remember," Jim cut him off, "I stand ready to be your friend too."

The two men went back to their discussion of the manufacturing process, when Romano suddenly bounded back into the warehouse. He had a look of satisfaction on his face.

"So?" Jim waved his hand.

"Well, a good case of vino makes for a happy inspector," Romano chuckled.

"Cheap price to pay," Jim said.

Romano turned to Murati.

"Does Mr. Marasco know everything he needs to know about the manufacture of synthetic drugs?"

"I believe he does," the Albanian responded with enthusiasm.

"Yeah, Armand is a wealth of information."

"Thank you for spending some time with me, Mr. Marasco," said Murati. "I'm always willing to discuss my end of the business."

As the two men left Armand Murati, the savvy Albanian looked a bit nervous.

The bastard better not rat on me, Jim thought.

It was not too long before the GPS locator David placed on John Gendusa's vehicle paid dividends. It was early afternoon on a sultry mid-August day when Gendusa moved the Escalade a short distance to the front entrance of the Marasco offices.

Once the GPS alarm fired, David hurried to the location to watch from a half-block away. He could see the car idling. In a few minutes, Tony bounded down the steps in a light tan summer suit, tie and pocket square. *You have to give it to the old guy,* David thought, *he knows how to play the part.* Undoubtedly, Gendusa had cooled down the car so his boss could enter a comfortable vehicle.

The vehicle moved through reasonably heavy Thursday afternoon traffic. David did not have to exert himself too much as the locator did its job by constantly flashing the Escalade's location. He could lag behind clearly out of view. The vehicle headed west on the I-10 expressway. When it was almost to the New Orleans Airport exit, it turned south on Williams Blvd coming to a stop at an attorney's office.

A fancy sign hung from a metal pole in the front landscaping of the white Georgian building. It read: Parker and Jones, Real Estate Attorneys. *Tony Marasco is no stranger to attorneys,* David thought, *but it looks like he may be selling or buying something.*

He waited at least a half-hour in the sweltering heat of his vehicle until Tony and Gendusa finally exited the attorneys' office. They were joined by a woman carrying a briefcase. She was impeccably dressed, well coiffed, and wore a lot of makeup. David could not help but notice that her skirt barely covered her ample assets.

Looks like this one is selling more than real estate, he thought.

The woman smiled warmly at Tony Marasco and shook hands with the two men. The batting of her false eyelashes added a large dose of sensuality. She then walked to her vehicle, a large, lumbering SUV.

It was obvious she was a high-rent real estate agent. David jotted down the license number. With a quick call to one of his police resources, he would soon find out who she was, and what company she represented. He hoped she might unwittingly spill some information on her client.

There is that old saying: "Fish and visitors stink after three days." Franco Romano had always enjoyed Tony's visits, but Tony's son was a pain in the ass. He was willing to put up with some of his drinking habits and shenanigans, but he didn't like the way he looked at his wife and was anxious for the annoying young man to return to the States.

Two more weeks, he fumed. *I can handle anything for two weeks.*

An unexpected phone call from Armand Murati, however, severely tested his patience.

"Hello Armand, how is everything?" Romano asked innocently.

The Albanian began the conversation with a dark tone.

"Franco, how long do you know this Jim Marasco? Is this a man that can be trusted?"

The question puzzled Romano.

"I have done business with his father for a very long time. Why do you ask me this? Did your time with him not go well?"

"It went well enough, I guess. He asked me a very unusual question."

"What did he ask?"

"He asked if I was treated well…by you."

"That son of' a bitch!" Romano seethed. He knew exactly what it meant. "Why would he say this?"

"It made me wonder…am I being tested…is he dirty. Maybe he was looking to create some tension…between us."

"How did you handle it?" the now irritated Romano shot back.

"Of course, I told him you and me…we have a very good relationship. He may have meant nothing by his comment, but I just thought you should know."

"You are right to tell me. This man is undermining me."

"You had better keep a good eye on him, my friend."

"Yes. And thank you very much for letting me know."

Romano hung up the phone.

What is this prick up to? he thought. *I have treated him like family…in my own house…and he goes behind my back.*

Romano stewed the entire night. Though Jim's conversation with Murati had done no long term damage, his lack of respect was growing old. Romano could be a patient man, and it took a lot for him to lose his temper, but when he did, he had ways to get even. He decided to keep this information to himself, and not challenge Jim. It was also the wrong time to bring this up with Tony; there was too much at stake.

Romano walked across the villa to the master suite. As he undressed, he saw the sleeping Bella in the king-sized bed. *She is even more beautiful when she sleeps.* He knew he was a fortunate man. He had a beautiful wife, wonderful children, and a great business. Now this rude and calculating asshole was making life miserable. He could not wait until things got back to normal. Jim Marasco was indeed skating on thin ice. The last thing Romano murmured before drifting off to sleep was, "Do not continue to try my patience, or things, for you, will not end well."

CHAPTER 19

❧

Harris was able to run the plates on the SUV David observed at the real estate attorney's office. The vehicle belonged to one Mary LeBlanc. David "Googled" her and found she was indeed a real estate agent. She worked for Savoy and Associates. He checked out the realtor's website, and a picture of the well dressed and over accessorized redhead was prominently displayed.

All these agent photos look the same, David thought. He smiled wryly. *Always taken five years earlier with a fair amount of airbrushing.*

LeBlanc had a fine track record. She was a member of the $25 Million Club, and she had recently been awarded a lifetime achievement award by the realtors' association for her service to home buyers and sellers.

David wanted to speak to the very successful Mary LeBlanc. At the same time, he knew he could easily tip off Tony Marasco. She had looked pretty chummy with him in the real estate attorneys' parking lot. *Maybe I need to buy some real estate,* David thought.

The next morning David showed up at the offices of Savoy and Associates under an assumed name. He handed a bogus card to the young receptionist.

"Welcome, Mr. Jones."

"I'm interested in speaking with one of your agents...about purchasing some property?"

"Do you have a specific agent in mind?"

"Um...Mary LeBlanc. I'm very impressed with her...her sales record. Would she be available?"

"Wise choice," the comely young woman said in a high-pitched voice. "I'll see if she has an opening."

"Please do."

After a few moments the receptionist returned bubbling.

"Mr. Jones, Ms. LeBlanc will be available in five minutes. May I get you a cup of coffee while you wait?"

"No thanks, I'm fine."

In short order, Mary LeBlanc sauntered out to meet her perspective customer. The red head walked like a contestant for Miss Universe.

This babe knows how to sell real estate, David thought.

"Hi, I'm Mary LeBlanc. How may I help you?"

"Yes, my name is Larry Jones. I'm interested in some commercial property."

The ever confident agent was quick to respond, "That's great, Mr. Jones, commercial real estate is my specialty."

David laughed to himself. *I bet whatever anyone asks about is her specialty. You gotta love sales people.*

LeBlanc invited David back to her spacious office. The walls were covered with framed achievements. Apparently she liked to display her record of success.

"Take a seat," she said pointing to an overstuffed chair. She pulled her own chair across from his.

"You got a lot of awards," David said pointing to the wall.

"I'm a busy girl. What type of commercial property do you have in mind?" she said, crossing her legs provocatively and tossing her red hair to the side. Her short skirt slid halfway up her thigh on cue.

David had to collect himself. He tried not to stare, but his eyes were out of control.

"Uh… what type of property?" David stammered. "Well, I'm a manufacturer's rep for a number of companies. I'm in need of office space and a large storage facility."

"Do you have a location preference?" LeBlanc asked in a sultry and somewhat dramatic voice.

"Umm…I guess it would be helpful if I was close to the airport, but I'd consider something across the lake as well."

"I know both areas very well. You're right up my alley," she said batting her fake eyelashes and turning to her computer. "What about a price range?"

"Hum… I'd like to be under 1.3 million," he suggested.

"You can't get much for that. It's on the lower end of the commercial range, but maybe I can work some magic."

Sure has a high opinion of herself, he thought.

"How 'bout you come sit next to me. I've got a few things I'd like to show you."

LeBlanc was a master of double entendre. She had a way of saying something innocent, while suggesting something erotic.

Watch yourself, David, he thought. *This gal's got danger written all over her.*

She spent more than a few minutes showing David some listings on her computer. It was apparent she relied on a large dose of perfume to aid in the sales process. Eventually, she asked if they could set up an appointment to view some properties.

David knew he had to make a move.

"Have you closed any recent sales of similar commercial properties?"

"Mr. Jones, I sell more commercial property in this area than…"

David interrupted, "I'd really like to talk to some of your clients as I finalize my decision on a realtor."

The woman, who had no shortage of self esteem, seemed surprised.

"Why, Mr. Jones, I closed a large transaction on a nice commercial property very recently. I can assure you, I will deliver what you want at a very competitive price."

Here's my opening.

"I mean no offense," David said, "but this is a big investment for me, and I want to make sure I touch all the bases." *Oh crap, now I'm speaking double talk.*

"The bases? I know I can ease your concerns."

"Would it be possible for me to talk to the client who recently purchased some commercial property?"

LeBlanc's demeanor became less forthcoming.

"Unfortunately, I am unable to do that. My most recent client does not want his purchase publicized."

David decided to back off.

"Okay, give me a bit of time to complete some additional research," David asked.

"Some of these nice properties will go quickly, Mr. Jones. I'd hate for you to miss out on a great deal."

Wow, she is persistent. David excused himself as gracefully as he could. As he walked down the hall, LeBlanc followed as though he were an insect crawling out of the web.

"Mr. Jones, I really am the best…at this type of thing. I certainly hope… to see you again."

After returning to his vehicle, David took a handkerchief and wiped the sweat off his brow. He decided it was time to call Alan Smith. Smith was lying low after the whole Marasco debacle, but he hadn't totally closed the door on providing some help.

The somewhat apologetic David cut right to the chase.

"Alan, this is David. I need your help."

"What's on your mind?"

"I've uncovered some potential information that may give us a clue as to Tony Marasco's next move."

"I'm listening, but I'm also hearing the words 'potential' and 'may'. That doesn't exactly cause me to ooze with confidence."

David laughed, but only halfheartedly.

"The information I've come up with might be very helpful, but I would need some FBI muscle."

"Go ahead, I'm all ears," Smith responded with a skeptical tone.

David went through all the details of his tail of Gendusa and Tony to the real estate law offices of Parker & Jones. He recounted his visit with the egotistical Mary LeBlanc. He was positive Marasco was buying some property, but LeBlanc had been careful not to disclose the name of her customer.

"Okay, he's buying property. So? Where does the FBI fit in?"

"I need information on the property involved in this real estate closing."

"What's so interesting about the property?"

"Alan, I believe it may have something to do with Marasco's drug business."

"Umm... possibly another bit of Marasco trickery."

"I'm convinced this is the potential break we've been looking for."

"Well," Smith said, "we could put some pressure on this Prima Donna."

"How?"

"There are federal laws that compel agents to disclose the names of those involved in real estate transactions."

"I was hoping that might be the case."

"The Patriot or Anti-Terrorism Act grants broad powers to law enforcement. Unfortunate it took something like 9/11 to give us the power we need."

"I appreciate that, but there's one problem with that approach."

"What's that?"

"If we beat down Mary Leblanc for information, Tony will know within minutes that we're snooping around."

"No doubt. I guess we're back to square one."

"Maybe not," the always resourceful David opined. "Wouldn't Parker & Jones be bound by the same disclosure restrictions as Mary LeBlanc?"

"I believe they would."

"Perhaps they will be inclined to give us the information confidentially. They have no reason to protect Marasco and expose themselves to possible disbarment and prison time."

"Good point, I say we make an appointment to visit Parker & Jones."

Planning for Marasco & Marasco's next shipment was proceeding on schedule. Tony and Romano discussed the specifics.

"Do you have the shipment date scheduled?" Tony asked his friend.

"Yes, the goods are scheduled to arrive in New Orleans on Monday September 3rd."

"No hang-ups, I hope. This has to go off without a hitch."

"Don't worry about hang-ups my friend," Romano bristled. "I've worked closely with Armand Murati to insure both the timeliness and quality of the 25i."

"I know you are all over this. Has Jim been helpful?"

There was a slight pause.

"He has been working side by side with me," he lied, knowing there was nothing to be gained by disclosing his frustration.

Jim had participated in the work and planning to some extent. But as was often the case, he began to grow restless and spent more time in the evenings out on the town, drinking and carousing with some of the locals.

None of this had a positive effect on Romano's opinion of Jim. It still stuck in his craw that Jim had tried to undermine his relationship with Murati. Romano was happy that Tony's new warehouse property had closed, and the necessary equipment was almost ready to handle the much anticipated shipment.

Trying not to be too obvious Romano asked, "When do you plan to have Jim return to the States?"

"I'd like him to stay at least through the final shipping preparation."

"That sounds okay." Romano again stretched the truth. "After we process and distribute the shipment, I'll put him on an airplane home."

"Good, that will be our plan."

It was obvious to Romano that Tony wanted John Gendusa to handle the next shipment's distribution from the new location, unencumbered by the antics of his son. He couldn't much blame him. *This guy has SCREW-UP written across his forehead,* Romano thought. *Thanks to God he is not my problem.*

⚜

Alan Smith and David arrived at the law offices of Parker & Jones at 9:00 a.m. sharp, just as the receptionist unlocked the front door. Smith asked to speak with the managing partner of the firm. In a matter of minutes, Donald A. Parker was shaking the hands of both men.

"Nice to meet you, Mr. Parker. We are here on official FBI business."

"FBI?"

"Yes!" Smith answered in his sternest FBI voice. "You may have closed on a real estate deal with criminal implications."

David could see the immediate impact on Donald Parker. It actually looked like the forty-something attorney was having a slight "panic attack". In seconds the attorney's nervous system seemed to send negative signals to his organs. Parker turned pale, his muscles tightened, and even his pupils enlarged. In a quaking voice he tried to respond.

"Gentleman…this is a first…for me. I hope I'm not being suspected of any illegal behavior."

"We're not making assumptions, Mr. Parker."

"I can assure you, the worst thing I've ever done was getting a speeding ticket." The nervous attorney's eyes averted their gaze.

Smith wanted the man to relax a little, but not too much. Parker's cooperation would be much better if he felt somebody else's skin was on the line, rather than his own.

"We're here to get details on a recent real estate transaction you closed. One of the realtors involved was a Mary LeBlanc."

"That was only a few days ago. I remember the transaction."

"Oh, I see," Smith said.

"I could get the closing statement and review it with you."

"That would be very helpful; we would certainly appreciate it." David played the good cop.

Parker's assistant brought in the closing documents to her still fidgety boss.

"Yes, this transaction was for the sale of a warehouse property in Hammond. The seller was a Peter King and the purchaser T & J Distributing."

"T & J?" Smith raised an eyebrow as he looked to David. He turned back to Parker. "Do you have the names of the corporate officers of T & J Distributing?"

"The file indicates that information is to remain private."

In his best FBI voice Smith pressed, "Mr. Parker, I am sure you are aware, money laundering and anti-terrorism financing regulations require those involved in a real estate transaction to collect this information and disclose it to federal authorities."

David kept a straight face as he wondered if Smith was playing a little loose with the truth. Regardless, the not so veiled threat worked immediately.

"The corporate officers are Anthony Marasco and James Marasco. They are also the sole owners of T & J Distributing," the attorney blurted almost breathlessly.

"T & J," David couldn't disguise a chuckle. "Tony and Jim."

"That's very helpful, Mr. Parker. We will also need a copy of the closing statement giving the location of the property."

"Uh… I'll get it for you right away."

"Oh! By the way, you must handle this visit and our discussion confidentially. I know you would never intentionally hinder an FBI investigation, but it's best I remind you of that."

"Don't worry, I don't plan to breathe a word. You can count on me, I'm a law abiding citizen. I also trust you would not disclose my cooperation to the Marascos."

"Pinky swear." Smith wiggled his little finger and rose to leave. He looked the attorney in the eye and said ceremoniously, "The FBI appreciates your service to your country."

As they walked back to Smith's sedan, David chided his resilient friend.

"I hope I'm never on the receiving end of Assistant Special Agent Smith's interrogation."

"Who, me?"

"Yeah, the guy folded like a cheap stadium seat."

Smith flashed an almost cocky smile.

It's good to have the old Alan back, David thought.

CHAPTER 20

⚜

John Gendusa was already spending virtually every waking hour at the Hammond facility. There were four trade contractors handling changes to the property that would accommodate the transfer of product from the balsamic bottles to the smaller 30 ML bottles used for street distribution of 25i.

The tradesmen were sent by one of Tony's construction contractor friends. Due to his many political ties, he was able to help his friend "win" a number of city contracts. In Tony's world of "one illegal deed deserves another," the mob boss knew he could count on his friend to get the work done on time and, most important, in secret.

Gendusa was not in a patient mood.

"Goddamnit! I'm not asking you to build the warehouse, simply make modifications."

"We movin' as fast as we can."

"It ain't fast enough! This place has to be ready day after tomorrow."

"We get it done."

"You better, you assholes. When I tell my boss the place will be ready, it damn well better be ready."

Gendusa meant business. He understood; this had to be a flawless and efficient operation.

As one might guess, there were more than workers present. Gendusa was leaving nothing to chance, and he had six of his best men onsite. One sat in a car at the entrance to the complex off of Old River Road. He was charged with monitoring any traffic that entered or left the location.

Gendusa told his lookout, "If so much as a goddamn squirrel comes down this road, you call me! Understand?"

"Nothin'll get by me, Boss."

"I'm countin' on it."

Another was stationed at the front sliding gate to the facility, three patrolled the perimeter, and one sat on a chair in a small office Gendusa typically occupied in order to shield himself from the heat and utilize the phone and computer.

❧

David knew he wouldn't have any help. He had to scout Marasco's new location. Alan Smith informed him the Bureau would not allow an FBI team to be directly involved in another raid, fearing a mistake would do irreparable damage to the local field office.

"Can you give me support?" David asked.

"The best I can offer is to have a team stationed nearby."

"Nearby? What good will that do?"

"Once you confirm the drugs are onsite, we can be on the property in minutes."

"Sounds like mop-up duty."

"I don't like it either, David." Alan shook his head and frowned.

"I guess the Bureau wants you to ride in like a white knight."

"Yep, we get the credit if you're right, and simply skulk away if you're not."

"Thanks for the honesty. Here's hoping I get to walk away."

"It stinks, David, but I've pushed as hard as I can."

"Understood, and I appreciate it."

David called on Detective Mark Harris to help complete the initial surveillance of the Hammond location. He knew his help might well be needed, depending on how heavily the place was fortified.

As they drove slowly down Old River Road, they immediately noticed a white Ford sedan parked on the shoulder of the entrance road. It would be impossible to simply drive past the vehicle into the entrance without being seen. David motioned Harris to drive past the turnoff and park.

"I think I can get by the vehicle," David said, "if you can distract the guy for only a few seconds."

David grabbed his binoculars and his digital/video camera.

"I'll be back within forty-five minutes, if everything goes according to plan."

"Got it. I'll take care of things on my end."

David crept into the cover of nearby woods and kept his eyes on Harris.

Harris pulled his vehicle off Old River Road and onto the two lane road leading to the warehouse. Not wanting the guard to get nervous and arouse his cohorts, Harris stopped his vehicle and walked over to the sedan where a lanky man sat smoking and reading the *Daily Racing Form*.

"Excuse me, I'm trying to find the Northshore Airport. It seems I've gotten myself turned around."

Harris could see he startled the guy. He stiffened and flicked some cigarette ashes off his pant leg.

"Man, don't be creepin' up on people like that."

"Sorry, didn't mean to startle you."

The man in the sedan took his fingers off his cell phone, apparently satisfied he simply had a lost schmuck on his hands.

"You need to go left on de River Road. Don't know the area too good myself. There's a gas station a ways back. Check with dem. Dey can hep you."

Mission accomplished! Harris signaled with a wave hidden behind his back.

"Thanks, I'll try that. Sorry to have bothered you."

Harris returned to his vehicle and turned it around in order to enter the Old River Road. The lanky man in the Ford sedan returned to smoking and reading his racing form.

David walked about one-hundred-and-fifty yards through trees and scrub-brush. He eventually positioned himself on a small rise about fifty yards from the warehouse. He moved slowly to the left shooting film of all four sides of the complex. To assess what they might face in the future, David counted the number of men standing guard over the location. Including Gendusa, he counted seven.

Place is well fortified, David thought. *Damn, I wish I had FBI support.*

If things worked as he hoped, David knew he would be back here shortly with an opportunity to shut down the Marascos and their drug business, once and for all. Planning had to be precise.

Gendusa wasn't the only one who would leave nothing to chance. Since the shipment was to arrive in less than two weeks, Tony remained in constant telephone contact. Though it was an hour's drive from Tony's residence to the Hammond facility, he insisted that he personally view the progress of the work.

Tony's driver took the elevated highway, which allowed passage through the Maurepas Swamp where Lake Pontchartrain and Lake Maurepas merged. Tony was not big on swamps.

"Who would live out here?" he said, as much to himself as the driver.

"Boss, this is big fishin' and huntin' territory."

"Shit, the place is filled with gators and god-knows-what else."

"I take it you're not a big fisherman." The driver laughed.

"Damn straight, I got better things to do with my time."

Tony dialed Gendusa to let him know they were only a few minutes away. He tried not to think about the ride back through the swamp that night.

Just as David began to make his way back to Harris and the car, he saw Gendusa come out of the small office. In moments, a blue Cadillac pulled into the complex. The driver got out first, and a well dressed man exited the back passenger side of the vehicle. It was Tony Marasco. The boss was coming to check progress at the facility.

Big man's here, David thought. *You're on Candid Camera, asshole.*

Gendusa shook Tony's hand, and they walked into the warehouse. David snapped a number of shots of both men on the premises. Later on, this would provide excellent documentation of Tony's knowledge of the operation and the work going on there.

David made his way back and entered Harris' vehicle.

"I see you had a visitor," Harris said. "The honcho is leaving no stone unturned."

David acknowledged with a smirk, "Yes, he's here to check on his investment, I'm sure."

"Great to catch him out here."

"Yeah! I got pictures. Smile for the camera, asshole," David said.

Rick Donner had provided updates from the Port on the ship's manifest. The information indicated the shipment would leave Genoa in four days and arrive in New Orleans after a seven day trek across the Atlantic. The goods were FOB--free on board--to their ultimate destination. The Commercial Invoice and Bill of Lading outlined the shipping contents and all other pertinent information. The freight forwarder and customs broker had filed the necessary paperwork confirming what was necessary to clear the product to its final destination.

David talked to Donner on the phone.

"Is the shipment still scheduled to arrive on the 3rd of September?"

"It is," the Port director replied. "Also, I reviewed the freight forwarding documents, and nothing is destined for Marasco's Tchopitoulas location."

"Interesting. No shipment to Tchoupitoulas Street, huh?" *Makes sense,* David thought. *The drugs are headed to Hammond in Tangipahoa Parish.* This time, the wily Marasco would be on the wrong end of the misdirection. David would be there and ready.

David drove to his Carrollton Avenue office to check mail and return a few phone calls. He thought to himself, *At some point, I need to get back to a case that actually pays money.*

The insurance investigation he solved had generated a tidy sum, but there were a number of other cases awaiting his attention. David climbed into the Camaro SS and headed to his Old Metairie home to spend an evening with Brenda and the boys. Things were about to heat up, and he knew he owed it to Brenda to let her know what was going on.

Everyone was in a good mood. The school year was getting cranked up, Brenda had her teaching assignment squared away, and the boys seemed to be ready for the start of the school year. Things were back to normal with Rob and Tim, as Rob chided his brother about living up to the reputation he had earned in high school.

"Better move your ass, if you intend to get a starting spot on the Varsity," Rob teased.

"Startin' spot? I expect to bat clean-up."

"No shortage of confidence, I see," said David.

Brenda laughed as she and David cleared the dinner table.

"You two All Americans finish your homework. You will have plenty enough time to aggravate each other."

Brenda and David relaxed on their family room couch with a glass of the wine left over from dinner. Brenda placed her feet on the coffee table and her head against David's shoulder. She enjoyed this time of the evening. It was one time when they could have some quiet, uninterrupted by a hectic schedule and parenting demands.

"Brenda, you know how I promised you I would keep my distance from the Marascos?"

"Yes! Aaand…" she answered abruptly, as if waiting for the inevitable other shoe to drop.

"I know when Marasco will receive his next drug shipment, and I know where."

"Will the FBI handle the bust?"

"That's the thing. Alan says he can have people stationed nearby. As soon as he knows the drugs are confirmed at the location, he has permission to move in. But otherwise…"

"I get it. They don't want to expose themselves to another PR nightmare…or a lawsuit. So you draw the short straw?"

"I won't be alone; Mark is willing to go in with me. It still galls him that John Cole was killed by the Marascos while under his watch."

Brenda shook her head and looked down at her lap.

"It's dangerous, David."

"Yeah."

He knew she hated to see him put in such a position of peril. But she knew from the beginning that he had chosen a dangerous career. The people he wanted to bring to justice had caused the death of their nephew, the murder of their nephew's friend, and the kidnapping of their own son.

"This might be the best…last chance to bring them to justice?" she whispered.

"That's what I'm thinking."

She looked him squarely in the eyes and said, "Then go kick their ass, David."

"I will, don't worry."

"Yeah sure, don't worry. If you don't come back to me safe, David Fournette, I'll…" she let the rest of the sentence trail off as a tear dripped into her wineglass.

CHAPTER 21

Things were very busy at Bella Ballerina. The shipment was being readied so it could be trucked the three hours from Cortona to Genoa, where it would be loaded onto a ship for its transatlantic crossing. Once Armand Murati completed the 25i manufacturing process, it was sent to a small, concealed bottling facility on the Bella Ballerina property, where it was bottled and labeled as Aceto Balsamica. Properly sealed as a finished product, it would not be detected by any of the normal methods employed by shippers, ports or government resources.

Romano was pleased with the product as he talked to Murati.

"This is your good stuff, my friend?" Romano asked.

"Certainly. There will be many Americans seeing strange visions," Murati laughed.

"We have this down to a science. I've changed the packaging."

"How is that?"

"No more Condimento. No use giving them any indication this might have some connection to drugs."

"I get it," Murati said, "a new delivery location and a new product description."

"That's right," Romano said with a tone of ultimate satisfaction.

Though there was great international publicity outlining the progress made against illicit drugs, the number of shipments was up dramatically. So there was, if anything, an increase in the amount of drugs reaching U.S. shores. In the case of a very organized and thorough operation like Franco Romano's, there was a very high chance of success.

After bottling and packaging was completed, the equipment was cleansed and a false wall was utilized to hide the small machinery. Within an hour, the clandestine operation became a simple storage facility, its true purpose never noticed by agricultural inspectors. The product was then loaded with Romano's legitimate product for the Port of Genoa.

Everything would have been perfect if Jim Marasco had not been involved. Murati and Romano had perfected the procedure, and Jim slowed the process down more than anything. Romano did not mind his inquiries, but the questions generally turned into commentary as to what might be a better or more economical way to handle the operation. Romano had to bite his lip when Jim constantly piped in.

"Time is money, Franco," he said. "The lower our costs, the higher our profits."

"So, now you educate me?" said Romano. "Your father has made a lot of money working with me."

"I believe that cuts both ways," Jim said unapologetically.

As the last of the crates were loaded on the truck, Romano resolved that Jim would never be invited back to his villa, much less involved in his business.

Though Jim would not return to New Orleans until this shipment was processed at the Hammond location, he would soon be out of Romano's hair.

The spent Romano took a deep breath and said, "I am ready to sit on my veranda, enjoy a nice pasto, a few glasses of vino, and the company of my Bella."

"I'm headed to town," said the always ready to party, Jim Marasco. He looked toward Murati who was doing some clean up. "What about you, Armand, do you want to join me?"

Romano had to turn partially away so his grimace was not visible.

The Albanian gave Jim his answer, "I'm afraid I will need to pass tonight, my young friend. I too have put in a long day's work."

"You must be kidding," mocked Jim. "You're talking like the old man. I thought you had more energy than that."

Murati shook his head and gave a barely audible and low nervous laugh, as one does when embarrassed as opposed to amused.

Romano turned to look at Jim. It was not so much what he said; it was how he said it. The diminutive winemaker could take some friendly teasing. In fact, he often poked fun at himself. But Romano felt Jim's tone was meant to denigrate the older man, and he did not appreciate it.

"Age has many benefits," Romano said.

"Really, tell me one."

"Older men tend to have the wisdom to think before they speak. Also, older men have many resources available to them. It may prove unhealthy to test them."

"I got plenty of time to sit around when I get old," Jim sneered. "Right now, I'm enjoying life." His deriding laugh proved Romano's subtle warning had fallen on deaf ears. "I'm off to town…my public waits."

As Jim exited the door, Murati looked at Romano and shook his head. "This man, he knows how to stir the shit."

"The bastardo is a piece of shit. Like most shit, he will rot."

Jim's evening at the local Cortona watering hole was somewhat similar to past outings, too much drinking and too many over-the-top advances to young women. The word had circulated that the wealthy and handsome young American had a dark side. One of the local girls had had an encounter with him a few weeks earlier. The young woman found herself in bed with Jim but was not prepared for the violence which he associated with sex. Her protests fell on deaf ears. She had reluctantly endured the brute that night so as not to further fuel his mean streak, but she had promised herself she would not be in that position again. In a small town like Cortona, rumors spread fast.

Now when Jim approached a woman, excitement was replaced with an understandable wariness. Alarm bells! Some of the local men had also come to the conclusion that it was preferable to buy their own drinks, than tolerate the boorish behavior of the drunken American.

Around 10:00 p.m. Jim decided the action had just about dried up. Unfortunately, his loss of interest in downtown Cortona was replaced by thoughts of the beautiful Bella Romano.

Wonder what that fine bitch is up to? he thought. *Probably bored stiff with the old man.* Fantasies ran rampant.

Since the night at Cibo, Jim had fought back the urge to aggressively pursue Bella. As was often the case with him, his memory was distorted from reality. All he could remember was the seeming calmness of Bella when he had placed his hand on her thigh. Somehow, he did not dwell on the fact she had ultimately rebuked his advances.

After staggering to his rented Alfa Romeo Giulietta, he turned the key and rocketed back to the Romano villa. As he traversed the winding roads to Bella Ballerina, Jim could not get the beautiful woman out of his mind. Good and sound reasoning was not utilized when there was something he wanted. He had grown up getting what he desired no matter the costs or consequences.

On most any other night, Jim's fantasies might have remained just that, but as luck would have it, Bella was in the kitchen when he entered the villa. She was washing a few glasses at the farmhouse sink when Jim came up to her from behind. She wore a red silk blouse and black stretch pants. She was the type of woman who possessed the same sexual allure when relaxing at home as when primping for a formal night on the town.

As he approached and put his hands on her waist, Bella cooed and threw her head back. When she turned, the somewhat startled woman gasped then greeted him warmly.

"You are home earlier than usual, Jim. Bad night on the town?"

"Yeah! Guess I'm getting bored with the Cortona nightlife."

"I can understand. We are a small town when compared to many places. Here we learn to love the natural beauty of the village and the countryside."

"Speaking of a natural beauty, you look fantastic…even when you are standing at a sink washing dishes."

"Thank you for the compliment," she whispered and gave him a seductive smile.

"A woman like you needs someone that can keep her satisfied."

Suddenly, Bella seemed to sense where this was headed, and she backed away. Earlier on, she had thought it somewhat flattering that the young American visitor showed an interest in her, but now she looked scared. It was apparent she should not give him further encouragement. That made her even more desirable in Jim's eyes.

"Did you not notice I have six children?"

Jim moved closer and placed his hands on her shoulders as she was backed into a corner.

"Franco is probably fast asleep," Jim slurred. "Let me show you…how a beautiful woman…should be treated."

Jim pulled her in and moved his face roughly against hers.

She flinched at the harshness of his kiss and his beard against her mouth and cheek.

"Please no…" Shocked, she attempted to pull away, but Jim held her firm in his grasp.

"Is this your little game?" he sneered. "Get a guy all worked up just to prove you can, and then shoot him down?"

"Jim…let me go, now! I'm a married woman who loves her husband and children. You have misjudged my intentions."

"Bullshit, you're just scared."

When she tried to pull away again, Jim's hand tore the top buttons of the red silk blouse exposing much of her breasts.

As Bella ran from the kitchen, Jim muttered, "Run to your old man, you stupid bitch. Who needs you anyway?"

⚜

As Bella entered the master bedroom, Franco Roman sat reading a magazine in one of the bedroom chairs. Though she tried to rush by him, he immediately sensed her agitated state. He rose and followed her into the bathroom.

"Bella, whatever is the problem?"

"Nothing, I simply tore my blouse as I was putting away the dishes."

"Bella, you have more blouses than any woman I know. Something else has you upset. Tell me, what is it?"

She sat down on her vanity chair and wiped the runny mascara from her eyes. He could see her tears.

"Franco, it is nothing. Forget it and we will go to sleep."

Romano pressed forward. "Let me guess, Jim Marasco?"

Bella failed to answer, but Franco knew he had struck a nerve.

"What did he do to you? You will tell me, Bella. I am your husband."

"Franco, he made a young man's mistake. It is only because he had too much drink."

"He is a no good bastard, drunk or not."

"Franco, you must promise me you will not make a scene in this house. I handled it."

Romano could not believe his circumstance. *What kind of animal is this man?* He felt there had been an issue between Bella and Jim the night they were at Cibo's for dinner, and he had seen how Jim looked at his wife. He also remembered the personal affronts he had suffered when Jim had belittled him in front of Armand Murati. For the most part, he had held his tongue and his temper, but attacking his wife could not go unpunished.

Romano reached down and touched the wife he loved more than anything.

"I promise you this, there will never be a scene in our home. But Jim Marasco will soon learn his lesson."

CHAPTER 22

❧

Agent Alan Smith was given District permission to place a team at the Louisiana terminal. His objective was to confirm the arrival of the Marasco shipments, pinpoint the disguised drugs, and ensure they were headed to Tony's Hammond facility. When these items were confirmed, David and Mark Harris would be notified to initiate their phase of the operation. David had agreed he would not go in until the product arrived at the facility with time to make sure it was actually 25i being rebottled for street distribution.

Smith would receive a go sign from David only when he and Harris had confirmed the drugs were in the Hammond warehouse. The FBI team and Alan Smith would be positioned on Old River Road ready to provide a quick response.

David understood the danger. He and Harris would need to somehow disarm the men in order to confirm the drug shipment was on the property. They would be out manned and out gunned. David's plan relied on his experience and the element of surprise.

It all seemed solid when they mapped it out, but David was well aware of Murphy's law: *If it can go wrong, it will.* They had been just as confident with their previous plan only to be outfoxed by the cunning of Tony Marasco. Anything left to chance would come back to haunt them.

David knew he and Harris would need to hold their positions until the truck had checked in and was cleared by the man Gendusa had stationed at the entrance to the Hammond industrial facility. The guard would notify Gendusa of the truck's arrival, and his failure to do so would surely cause them to abort the acceptance of the product.

On the morning of September 3, 2012, Rick Donner had talked with Smith to advise him the shipper, Italia Oceana, had indeed arrived at the Louisiana Avenue Terminal. The goods were being off loaded, and it was expected that ground pickup and delivery of the 25i would take place in the early afternoon.

Smith called David with the news.

"David, this is Alan. So far so good. The shipment arrived right on schedule."

"That sounds fine, Alan. Harris and I will listen for your updates as you track the delivery. As soon as the goods are cleared by the guard, we'll be prepared to move."

There was an eerie sense of Déjà vu as David waited for the ground transport of the drug shipment. He did his best to dismiss the negative thoughts.

This time will be different, he hoped. *Tony Marasco spent a great deal of money on his Hammond purchase…this has to be it!*

Tony Marasco was pleased to hear of the arrival of the Bella Ballerina goods. He talked to Gendusa by phone.

"Notify me the minute you receive the shipment in Hammond."

"No problem, Boss, I intend to."

"Everything is riding on this," Tony warned. "We can't waste time."

Tony understood the street was restless. His trickery and deceit had de-livered a crushing blow to the FBI's investigation, but it had done nothing to appease his distributors who were clamoring for product. More importantly, it had done nothing to put money in his pocket.

Tony planned to have the 25i rebottled and ready for distribution by the end of the day. Once that was accomplished, things would be back to normal. He also knew he would be calling Jim to return home, and he was hopeful his time in Italy with Franco Romano would help his attitude and their relation-ship. He needed to have the old Jim back. He was not getting any younger, and the stress of managing numerous illegal businesses had taken its toll. Such an operation could never be passed outside the family.

⚜

Franco Romano also knew time was running short. He had come to the conclusion that continuing a relationship with Marasco was a long shot. He could see the handwriting on the wall. One day Tony would be out of the picture, and his son would take on even more of the day to day activities of the business.

That would not happen, if Romano had anything to say about it. Trust was everything to the old Italian, and he had none when it came to Jim. It took all of his willpower to honor the commitment he had made to Bella. Though he did not create any strife in the villa, Romano barely talked to Jim, and engaged him in conversation only on the rare occasions when they had a conference call with Tony.

On the afternoon of September 3rd, Romano called an old friend, Tommaso Basso.

"Tommaso, this is Franco. I may need a favor from you."

Basso seemed happy to hear Romano's voice. He had been helped many times by the wine maker, and Romano had stood behind him when he had faced a long sentence in an Italian prison. Fortunately for Basso, Romano had the connections and the money to hire the best lawyers. As a result, Romano had made a friend for life, the type of friend that would do most anything in return.

"How can I be of service, my dear friend?"

Like clockwork, the independent motor carrier arrived at the Louisiana Avenue Wharf to accept the designated cargo from the Port. Tony had paid the facility for full loading, so Port personnel loaded the merchandise from the dock to the truck. By 2:00 p.m. the truck was rolling through the gates of the terminal on its way to the north shore of Lake Pontchartrain.

Monday afternoon traffic was always reasonably heavy, and Agent Smith had properly anticipated it would take about one-and-a-half hours for the truck to arrive at the Hammond complex off of Old River Road.

"They're rolling, David."

"Sounds good. Everything look to be in order?"

"From what we can tell. We'll be in touch," Smith added.

Through effective "tailing" techniques, the shipment would never be out of direct visual contact of the FBI. Armed with the knowledge the truck was, in all probability, headed to Hammond helped with the floating box system the team utilized, but they also remained on high alert for any change in routing.

David received constant updates as the vehicle made its way out of New Orleans and west on the I-10 expressway. This was what he disliked most: *waiting!* He constantly ran the plan through in his mind. As each stage of the anticipated assault on the facility played out, his muscles seemed to tense and relax, as if subconsciously developing the necessary muscle memory to carry out the plan.

Hurry up and wait, David thought, *the story of my life.*

At exactly 3:35 p.m. Smith sent an encrypted radio alert to David and Harris. The truck would be pulling off Old River Road in approximately two minutes. By the time the message completed, David could see the large cargo van switch on its right turn signal to enter the access road. The guard exited his car and approached the van. After a few seconds, the van was cleared to proceed to Marasco's facility.

David watched as the guard radioed the tuck's arrival to John Gendusa.

Gendusa stood outside of the office as the truck came through the gate. He was fully prepared with five armed associates at the ready, as well as the three men who were responsible for the rebottling process. Though he felt some sense of relief that the shipment had arrived safely, it was now his job to see that the 25i was converted for street distribution as quickly and efficiently as possible.

Gendusa instructed his men, "Unload the truck the minute it comes to a stop."

"We got it, Boss."

"And be damn careful. All I need is for this shit to be splattered all over the place."

He had told his men to be discreet when they unloaded the truck, so the clueless transportation company and its truck could be released. He didn't want additional eyes and ears wondering what was going on with the balsamic crates. If everything went as scheduled, Gendusa planned to have the entire shipment repackaged by 7:30 p.m. Tony Marasco was adamant that he wanted the process completed, so they could began distribution the following day.

The bottle transfer was no simple task. Any spillage amounted to hundreds, possibly thousands of dollars down the drain. The Marascos had learned through experience and invested in a closed system which allowed for the easy and safe transfer of the expensive liquid. Each bottle had a cap and connector. When the connectors from each bottle were joined, a seamless transfer could be made.

Though the process minimized loss due to spillage, it remained somewhat labor intensive and slow. Rushing the process was counterproductive. By working efficiently, Gendusa felt they could meet the designated timeframes.

When the empty cargo van left the complex and turned away, it was time for David and Harris to move. Smith and the FBI task force stationed themselves a quarter-mile from the Old River Road entrance; they would remain there until radioed by David.

Harris pulled his vehicle onto the shoulder of the access road. This caught the guard's attention, but Harris made no attempt to turn into the entrance. It did create enough of a distraction that David was able to move around to the rear of the vehicle from the trees. Working with precision, he approached the driver's open window. With one fluid motion, he applied a crushing blow to the man's left temple, and a concentrated dose of chloroform went across the unlucky lookout's nose. In less than a minute, the man was completely disabled.

In mere seconds, Harris was at the vehicle. He bound the man, grabbed his keys, and placed him in the trunk of the sedan.

Both men moved silently along the trees lining the left side of the road.

"Mark," David said, "I'm going through the trees to the back of the warehouse. You stay down until I signal you to move toward the guard at the gate."

It took David approximately fifteen minutes to move from the road's edge to the rear of the warehouse facility. Though he traversed the uneven terrain like a shadow, because of his heightened senses, the sound of the dry pine needles and twigs seemed to snap and reverberate as he moved.

It was now 6:15 p.m. and the tall pine trees had already begun to cast a shadowy pall over the facility. The dappled colors of twilight and the breeze through the trees caused a sense of movement when there was none. It played tricks with David's mind, but he remained focused on gaining silent entry to the facility and maintaining the element of surprise.

With minimal effort, David used his wire cutters to create an opening in the chain-link fence. He squeezed through the small opening and within seconds was crouched against the warehouse's rear wall.

He whispered a message to Harris through his radio transmitter.

"I'm inside at the rear. How many men at the front?"

Harris muttered, "I count three at the front of the warehouse."

"Can you see if Gendusa is in the yard?"

"That's a negative. He's in the office, and there's a man at the office door."

"Give me exactly two minutes, then move on the guard at the gate."

David moved in crouched paces up the side of the warehouse and positioned himself behind a stack of pallets approximately ten feet from the left front corner. He tossed a stone from the gravel-covered yard against the metal wall drawing the attention of the man stationed at the left front of the building.

The lookout tossed a cigarette to the ground, removed his weapon from its holster, and moved cautiously toward the noise. As he neared the stack of pallets, David threw his left elbow into the man's Adam's apple and almost simultaneously drove the butt of his Glock semi-automatic pistol into his nose. Blood gushed from the man's face, and he immediately fell to his knees and then onto his stomach. David pulled him behind the pallets and positioned himself at the left front of the warehouse.

One down and at least six more to go, he thought. His adrenaline pumped and he sucked air in quick breaths.

One of the two remaining men stepped just inside the door which gave David only a few seconds to reach the man whose back was facing him. Hearing the muffled and quick-moving steps, the unsuspecting thug turned only to have David's heel firmly thrust into his solar plexus. The noise startled the man inside the door. As he drew his weapon, David dropped to his knee and pulled the trigger of his Glock 22, striking the third man in the upper right chest.

185

Harris was on the gate guard at the same moment as the report of David's pistol reverberated through the air like a grenade.

"Take that dipshit," he said, striking the guard in the back of his head with the butt of his weapon.

Before he could redirect his attention to the guard stationed at the office near Gendusa, a thud rattled Harris's left shoulder. He felt a burning sensation, but responded by instinct, squeezing off a shot. As the office guard moved toward him on a dead run, Harris dropped him in his tracks.

"Are you okay?" David yelled.

"Flesh wound…I'm…I'm okay."

"Where's Gendusa?"

"In the office?" Harris answered.

Upon entering the building David could clearly see that the rebottling process had been in full swing. *It's 25i, all right.* He motioned the wounded Harris to guard the three unarmed men who were packaging the product. He then transmitted a message to Alan Smith.

"Confirmed 25i…move in…full alert…we do NOT have Gendusa!"

David moved toward the office. The door was half open, but he kicked it open with his Glock at the low ready position. A quick scan revealed nothing.

"Where the hell did he go?" David shouted.

Suddenly Harris cried out, "Moving toward the rear!"

David ran along the side of the warehouse. As he reached the edge of the building, he cautiously peeked around the corner. He could barely see Gendusa's silhouette due to the advancing darkness.

What is he doing? Straining to see, it became apparent the hulking man was trying to squeeze through the rear fencing at the same place where David had entered. He looked like a fat rat in a trap.

"Stop, or I'll shoot!" David yelled.

Since he was partially restrained by the chain link fence, Gendusa obeyed the order and dropped his weapon.

David moved cautiously toward him.

"Get your hands up, and hit the ground face first."

"Just let me get out of this fence," Gendusa begged.

The massive Gendusa moved slowly as if to extract himself from the fence, but in one motion, he pulled a small Rugar from his rear waistband.

In the briefest of seconds, David saw the flash of metal and immediately fired. His shot penetrated the right side of Gendusa's stomach.

"I'm not done, you bastard!" Gendusa yelled.

Marasco's key lieutenant grasped his gut with one hand and went down to one knee, but he was able to get off a quick shot that whistled by David's ear.

David's next shot hit him square in the forehead.

Gendusa's face lost all expression. As the gun dropped from his hand, he immediately fell face first into the dirt.

"You're done now…you piece of shit!" David yelled out.

FBI Special Weapons and Tactics team rushed into the complex, and Agent Smith watched as David knelt by the body and confirmed Gendusa was dead.

In a matter of minutes the FBI chemist confirmed the presence of 25i.

The ecstatic agent pronounced, "This time the Marascos won't escape justice."

After securing the area and the contraband, Smith radioed FBI support personnel who were guarding the Audubon residence of Tony Marasco.

"Don't let anyone enter or leave the residence. We will be there in short order to make the arrest."

CHAPTER 23

❧

Jim Marasco was ready to go home. He planned to depart from Cortona once Romano received confirmation that the shipment had been converted and distributed. He could sense the aloofness of Bella, who avoided him like the plague, and the cold shoulder of Franco Romano, who was barely speaking. Apparently Romano had not appreciated his business acumen, and Bella had not fallen under his spell. Both left him wondering, *They just stupid or jealous?*

There were no more celebratory glasses of wine or joint meals with the Romanos. Basically, Jim stuck to his routine, a little work at the winery by day and a little debauchery at night. This particular evening, his luck seemed to be improving. Just about the time he felt he had struck out at the local bar, a pretty, young Italian woman, no more than twenty-five years old eyed him from a table across the room. The green light was more than obvious. In less than an hour she was entwined in his clutches. As he stared into her beautiful, dark eyes, he found her kisses warm and wet.

"Maybe I should ask your name," Jim chuckled.

"Gabriela," she cooed. "And you?"

"Just call me Jim. May I ask where you are from?"

"I live in Rome. Just here for business. Shall we have some more wine?"

"By all means."

The young woman became more amorous as the night wore on. Jim was infatuated with the ringlets of black, curly hair that framed her face and tossed wistfully every time she moved. Her red dress hugged her body and showed ample curves. His wandering hands explored everything he could reach and met no resistance.

These olive-skinned women know how to seduce a man, he thought.

"You said business. What do you do?" Jim asked out of curiosity. "Besides make out in bars, that is."

"Sales Director. I work for the Villa Piazza Hotel chain. There is one just down the street."

"Yes, I know it well," he smirked. *Must be my lucky day.*

"I love my work." She reached under the table and pulled his hand further up between her legs.

"Why haven't I seen a pretty thing like you in here before?"

"My job occupies much of my time, but when I do get out, I like to have a good time."

"Perhaps we could find a place to get to know each other a little better."

"My job has a few nice benefits…"

"Yeah, tell me about 'em," Jim interrupted.

"For one, I have a very nice suite."

"Well, Gabriela, I suggest we make good use of it. Let's get the hell outta here!"

They left Jim's rental car at the bar and walked the two blocks to Gabriela's hotel. The young woman laughed and kissed him as they entered the lobby, leaving no doubt he was soon going to have a fine Italian farewell. The hotel room door had barely closed behind them when Jim grabbed her from behind and hiked up the red dress. She turned and accepted him with desperate and eager arms. The kisses were harsh as his big hands moved roughly over her body. Clothes flew all over the room. He swept her up in strong arms and threw her across the bed like a rag doll.

The sex was rough, fast and furious, but to his surprise, the girl appeared to enjoy his brutal assault. Spurred into action he yanked her hair to one side and slapped her across the face.

"Come on," she laughed, "is that all you got?"

He grabbed her by the throat and thrust into her will all his might.

"Take that, you whore!" he shouted.

She responded with guttural screams in a crescendo of heightened pleasure.

Soon, they both lay spent on the king-size bed.

"Too bad…I didn't meet you…earlier," he said, trying to catch his breath. "I think we would be good together."

"Yes?" she replied.

"Unfortunately, I will be leaving Italy in the next few days."

The flirtatious young woman propped herself up on one elbow and looked him in the eyes. She licked a drop of blood from the crack in her lower lip and spoke in reasonably fluent English

"You know what they say, it is not how long the music lasts, it is the quality of the melody. I think…we make good music."

Jim looked at his watch. It was almost 2:00 a.m. and tomorrow was the big day.

"I hate to say this, Gabriela, but I need to head out. I have a busy day tomorrow."

"But I have the room all night."

The young woman still lying on the bed displayed an exaggerated, pouty face. For once, after such violent sex, he hated to leave. He got out of bed and quickly dressed.

"If you must, then go, but I do hope you will remember Gabriela." She rose from the bed and kissed him.

He held her for only a second, and unceremoniously left the room. He could hear the door close behind him and the click of the safety lock. *Wow!* he thought. *That's my kinda woman. Maybe I shudda got her number.*

Jim made his way back across the plaza to the rented Alpha Romeo. He smiled at his good fortune. He had scored big on what could be his last night in Cortona. He would soon be rid of Franco Romano and that stuck-up broad, Bella.

To hell with them, Jim thought, *I'm goin' home.*

Tomasso Basso watched Jim from afar. He had been watching him as he spent the hours in the bar with the young Italian woman. He watched him walked her to the hotel. *I hope it was all worth it,* he thought. Now he watched him walk back to his car.

Jim was obviously drunk and spent as he staggered across the parking lot. He leaned down in the dim light and fumbled for his car keys. Finally, he managed to open the driver's side door and settle into the seat behind the wheel. He shook his head side to side, as if to shed his drowsy state.

Basso put his fingers in his ears and watched the brilliant flash as Jim Marasco turned the key.

The explosion broke the calm of the early morning and rocked the entire downtown area. Basso scurried away into the darkness. He shrugged and thought, *My young friend, you pissed off the wrong man.*

Angela Marasco sensed that her husband was under a high level of stress. She had no idea what was going on and knew better than to ask. At 9:00 p.m. when the doorbell rang, she jumped with a start. Tony shouted from the study for her to, "Answer the goddamn door!" She had a bad feeling as she walked across the cold marble and opened the door just a few inches. She saw three men in suits standing on her front porch. As she tried to close it, one man stuck his foot in and forced it wide open.

Angela gasped. She stood shivering by the cut-glass door and asked, "How…may I help you?"

Assistant Special Agent Alan Smith flashed his FBI credentials and said, "Mrs. Marasco, we have a warrant to take custody of your husband."

Angela could feel the color drain from her face. It seemed the years of self denial were crumbling around her. Though she always had doubts about Tony's business, his self assurance and air of invincibility helped suppress long-held concerns.

Hearing the commotion, Tony walked out of his study, and faced the men. He seemed to recognize them. Angela panicked when she saw a cold chill grab his facial expression. For one split second, she felt the type of palpable fear when one realizes she could lose everything, including her freedom.

Tony's years of managing crises and narrow scrapes allowed him to quickly regain his composure.

"To what do I owe this visit, Agent Smith? I thought you might have been relieved from duty by now, due to your stupidity."

"I'm afraid I'm still very much a part of the FBI. Unfortunately for you, Mr. Marasco, you are being placed under arrest on drug smuggling and distribution charges…and the murder of John Cole."

As Smith spun him around roughly and put on the cuffs, Tony looked toward David with a sneer. "I see the FBI now needs a two-bit detective to handle their business."

"I wouldn't have missed this for the world," David answered. "Sure feels good to see a murdering bastard…a kidnapper and a crook…go down in flames."

"One would think you might have learned a lesson by now, Fournette."

"Your threats won't work anymore, Marasco, you're going away for a long time."

Tony eyed David with disdain.

"Angela, get my attorney on the phone and tell him to meet me at the FBI detention facility. Get a message to Jim. Tell him to stay put until he hears from me."

"But, Tony, what…"

He cut her off, "Agent Smith, you do realize, I'll be out before you get a good night's sleep."

"Right now, all I know is, you'll be taken into custody, photographed and fingerprinted. Then, you'll again be Marandized and given the opportunity to give a voluntary statement. We've done our job and we've got a shit-load of evidence. Now we leave it to the court to do theirs."

Angela felt lightheaded as she put Tony's sport coat over his shoulders. Seeing her husband in cuffs was more than she could bear. He had been arrested many times, but this time seemed different. She began to wonder about her own fate.

"Tony, tell me…this is all a big mistake, right? What do I tell Jim…when I reach him?"

"Tell him these clowns got the wrong man. Tell him to stay in Cortona for now. I'll be home by tomorrow morning."

Angela closed and locked the door. Suddenly she didn't feel like the attractive, middle-aged, blond aristocrat role, she had so enjoyed playing. Fear racked her brain and stress caused her fingers to tremble as she dialed her son's cell phone. The phone rang, but there was no answer. Believing she must have dialed incorrectly, she again dialed his number getting the same response.

She sat down and balled. Both the men in her life were gone. Her husband in custody and her son thousands of miles away, she felt truly vulnerable and alone.

Angela cried out in desperation, "How could this get any worse?"

CHAPTER 24

❧

Agent Smith did his best to isolate Tony Marasco before his attorney arrived.

David stood in the darkened room and watched the interrogation through a one-way mirror. He understood the questioning would be handled by the FBI. Tony was obviously uneasy, but the bravado he worked years to perfect helped maintain an air of arrogance and superiority. David laughed to himself. It was pure heaven to see Tony Marasco sweating bullets.

The interrogation room was brightly lit, and Tony could see only his own reflection, Alan Smith and Andy Hammond, the Special Agent in Charge. The stark and confined room was designed to be a very uncomfortable place.

Now that Hammond saw the potential for a big time narcotics bust and the conviction of a well known New Orleans crime boss, he was only too happy to have the FBI front and center. As a matter of fact, he had announced a press conference the following afternoon. He was a rising star and had been promoted from the Baltimore Field Office where he was an assistant to the Special Agent in Charge.

Hammond looked FBI from head to toe: well trimmed blond, wavy hair, thin black tie and rugged good looks. He also carried himself with a cockiness that helped mask some level of insecurity. His manicured appearance, impeccable suit and starched shirt gave evidence he was not one of the leaders who had worked his way up from the front lines.

Hammond could be called Mr. Ambitious. He was the type who could not wait for the next promotion, even if he still had areas to master in his current assignment. Mainly, he was concerned about getting to the top. Putting the bad guys away was a means to an end.

Tony Marasco had no idea John Gendusa was dead, and the agents intended to use that lack of knowledge to their advantage.

"Your boy, Gendusa, is singing like a birdie," Smith said. "We have every stitch of evidence necessary to convict you on multiple counts of drug distribution and money laundering under the RICO Act."

"I don't believe you...you're full of shit!" Tony blurted.

"You are also being fingered as the individual who authorized a hit on the young Tulane student, John Cole."

Tony shook his head and looked puzzled.

"John Cole? Who's that? What would I have to do with murdering a student?"

"You knew John Cole was the only link to the overdose your son gave to Billy Brewer," Hammond chided. "And you had him eliminated."

"Under the RICO Act," Smith added, "you can be charged even if you didn't personally commit the crime, because you are the head of a criminal enterprise."

"I am a legitimate importer and taxpayer, and a law abiding citizen. You guys work for me."

"That's a crock and you know it. You need to come clean, Marasco, or you're going away for life," Alan snarled with his face only inches away.

Tony fidgeted uneasily in the hard, straight-backed interrogation room chair. David noticed a quick shift in his facial expression. Their questions were having some impact.

"John Gendusa has worked for me many years…he would never sell out his boss."

"That's where you're wrong," Hammond said. "A man will do anything if he thinks a plea deal will keep him from a murder-one conviction."

Smith stood, leaned forward and placed his hands flat on the table. Invading a suspect's space was one tried and true way to ratchet up the pressure. David could sense a growing tension on Tony's face. The old man lowered his gaze.

"I'm not talkin'," he said, "Get me my lawyer."

"You have one chance to tell us the truth about John Cole, or we offer Gendusa the deal." Hammond sneered in anger.

David saw Jeremy Givens storm through the hallway toward the interrogation room. The lawyer had stood side by side with the Marascos during Jim's potential indictment, and he had long been on retainer whenever their business dealings brought potential heat from the law. The tall, thin man's long grey hair, angular features and flashy clothing gave him a quirky and intellectual aura that played well with juries. He was considered somewhat shifty, but no one could demean his capabilities. Prosecutors hated facing him, because he could and would use every sleazy trick in the book to undermine the prosecution's case. He demanded to be admitted to the interrogation room and stormed in.

"Mr. Marasco, do not say anything further. Gentlemen, my client has the right to meet confidentially with me before any questioning, and I will be present in any future interrogations."

"You better talk some sense to your client. He'll never see freedom again unless he cooperates," Hammond said in exasperation as he and Smith walked out of the room.

"Mr. Marasco doesn't need your legal advice…that's why he has me," Givens responded.

David watched like a fly on the wall. Givens quickly determined Tony Marasco hadn't made any incriminating statements involving John Cole's death. He also broke the news to Tony that Gendusa would not be talking to anybody.

"He took a bullet between the eyes," the lawyer said.

Tony turned his head away to collect himself. He had lost his loyal lieutenant and his best and most trusted friend. On the other hand, he seemed pleased Gendusa turning state's evidence was nothing but an FBI ruse.

Givens told Tony he could beat any charge relating to Cole's "accident" but advised there was an uphill battle on the counts of international smuggling, drug distribution and money laundering. The arresting body and prosecutor had the right to keep Tony for at least seventy-two hours, and they were already in process of filing the appropriate motions with the Federal Court to hold Tony until there was a bail hearing.

"You're not going to get out of detention. The authorities have significant evidence on the rest of the charges. Our best bet is to see if we can get a speedy bail hearing."

The proud man was not the type to break easily.

"Then let's get to work. You need to get me out of here."

David heard a noise behind him.

"Hey David, what are you doing in there?" Smith said, closing the door behind him.

"Who me?" David asked.

"You know about attorney-client privacy. You're not allowed to listen in."

"Oh yeah," David said. "I guess we better go."

⚜

Angela Marasco spent a restless night. Givens indicated she would be able to see Tony sometime the next morning, but he wasn't going free. The tired and confused woman went through the motions of readying herself. As she poured a cup of coffee, she began to worry why she was unable to reach Jim.

Remembering Tony's instructions as he was being led off by the FBI, she decided it might be best to call Franco Romano. Certainly he would be able to get her in touch with Jim. She placed an international call to Cortona.

"Mr. Romano, this is Angela Marasco, Tony's wife."

"Mrs. Marasco? How nice. Oh, oh well, how are you?"

"Not well, I'm afraid."

"Sorry for my surprise. I was expecting a call from Tony."

"I hate to bother you, but we have a problem here in New Orleans, and I can't get in touch with Jim."

"But Tony? What about Tony?"

"Mr. Romano, the FBI has taken Tony into custody. I don't know what the hell is going on, but he asked me to call Jim. Jim's not answering his phone."

Long pause.

"Mr. Romano?"

"Jim?" Romano sounded confused.

"Yes, Jim, you know, my son? He's been working with you?"

"Of course. Last night he said he was heading to town for dinner and drinks with friends. He did not come back to the villa last night."

"And?"

"Don't worry. Probably sleeping it off somewhere. When he arrives, I will tell him to call you immediately."

"Jim's missing?" she asked in alarm.

"No, no, not missing, I expect to see him soon. What about Tony?"

"Last night FBI agents took Tony away. They claim he's involved in some drug ring or something."

"That is ludicrous! Do they have any proof?"

"Tony said not to worry, he would be released this morning. But…but he hasn't come back. How can I not worry? I have a husband in jail, and I can't reach my son."

"I can see what you are dealing with, Mrs. Marasco. Concentrate on helping your husband. I will look for Jim and have him call you."

"Please, I'm worried sick."

"Certainly, he is fine, simply enjoying the company of friends. As soon as I find him, I'll put him in touch."

"Thank you...thank you and goodbye."

Romano's mind raced. If the FBI had hard evidence, he could well be implicated. He didn't want to raise Angela's suspicions about Jim, but he was obviously concerned about his own skin. Jim Marasco was toast, and this would not be a good time for investigations. His ass was on the line. If the authorities came calling, it would not be his friends with the local municipal police, but rather the federal Guardia di Finanza. He knew the shipments could easily be traced back to his operation. It was time to conceive a full-throttled defense.

Romano thought of Angela with absolutely no remorse for the Marascos. Their son was a complete asshole who violated his wife under his own roof. Now, Tony's "full proof plan" had seemingly disintegrated.

Now, my friend, Romano thought, *it is every man for himself.*

CHAPTER 25

Cortona was abuzz with speculation. The picturesque town had not seen anything like this in recent memory. It didn't take long to confirm the blast was caused by a powerful bomb activated when the vehicle's ignition switch was turned. The violent explosion had all the earmarks of an assassination. Though it looked to be a targeted kill, the Federal police could not completely rule out some form of terrorism until the remains of the victim were identified.

Through good forensic work, the Italian authorities were able to confirm the vehicle identification number. Then the automobile was traced back to a local car rental agency. The vehicle involved was one of the more expensive rentals, and the rental agency was able to determine it had been rented to an American by the name of James Marasco.

Forensic testing was also completed on the deceased's personal possessions. Jim's passport was completely charred, but utilizing magnification imaging of what remained, the examiners confirmed the last name. Paperwork at the rental agency also disclosed the customer was staying at the villa of a Franco Romano on the property of Bella Ballerina Winery.

Of course, the authorities had no idea who killed the young American or why. They contacted Franco Romano, but they also faced the task of notifying the U.S. State Department, standard procedure for an American who died abroad as the result of a crime.

When the doorbell rang, Franco Romano answered it himself. It wasn't unexpected.

"Mr. Romano. We are from the Federal police."

"Police?"

"I'm afraid we have some bad news," the man said in a subdued and respectful tone.

"Don't tell me this has something to do with my houseguest?" Romano said.

"An American, Jim Marasco, was killed last night."

"Killed? How did it happen?"

"Vehicle explosion, a bomb was triggered by the ignition system in his car."

"My God! You must be kidding. Who would want to harm this young man?"

"That is our question of you." The investigator looked at Romano with some skepticism. "Do you have any idea who might desire to do him harm?"

Yeah, at least a couple of dozen people I know, Romano thought.

"Why, no. He has only been here a short time."

"One must ask, why no missing person's report?"

"Well, I…"

"Didn't you think something was wrong when he failed to return to your villa?"

"Yes, I was somewhat alarmed, but this is not the first time he has stayed out."

"What do you mean, Mr. Romano?"

"Jim liked to hang out at the Cortona night spots. He loved the young women, and he slept out a number of times before." He thought quickly how to cover his ass. "I notified the local police this morning that we could not locate him. As a matter of fact, his mother called looking for him, because he wasn't answering his cell phone."

"And the police…what did they say?"

"Not much. They said it would be a day or two before they would act."

"May I ask why the young man was staying with you?"

"He is the son of an American business associate. I sell him wine and balsamic. He wanted his son to learn more of the wine-making business."

The obvious follow up question came next.

"Mr. Romano, you were his host. Are you positive you saw no conflict between this Marasco and anyone?"

"I have heard rumblings that he made a few enemies in the bars."

"Why would that be?"

"He liked to party and he had a fairly aggressive personality. He was also very aggressive with the young ladies. Maybe a boyfriend…or lover, no?"

"We are already canvassing those who had contact with him."

"Can you think of anything else, Mr. Romano?"

"Well, his father did tell me he had a few scrapes with the American authorities. Thought I would be a good influence…or something like that."

"Scrapes?"

"He got in a lot of trouble, it seems. I assume he had enemies in America."

"Perhaps this trouble followed him here?"

"Perhaps."

"Please, let us know if you hear anything at all." The inspector handed Romano his card.

Three days after the explosion, Angela Marasco answered a call on the family's home telephone from a representative of the State Department's Bureau of Consular Affairs. It was their responsibility to notify the next-of-kin, when a United States citizen died abroad.

When the phone rang, Angela literally ran for it. She hadn't had any news and Romano wouldn't return her calls.

"Hello, my name is Robert Anderson. I'm with the State Department. May I speak with either Mr. Anthony Marasco or Mrs. Angela Marasco?"

"This is Angela," she replied.

"Mrs. Marasco, we have some very unfortunate news. Your son, James, died in a vehicle explosion in Cortona, Italy."

"What? What are you talking about?" She couldn't comprehend the message. *Not possible,* she thought

"Representatives from the Bureau of Consular Affairs will be making a personal visit to your residence to provide complete details and assistance, but we try to notify next-of-kin as quickly as possible when faced with a tragedy like this."

Angela's hands were shaking. She had trouble holding onto the phone. It suddenly felt as though it weighed a hundred pounds. In an almost robotic trance she made her way to the club chair in the kitchen's hearth room. She heard the words, but there was a sense of disbelief. She felt a stabbing pang like she had never felt before.

"You must be mistaken. I spoke only two days ago with the man Jim is staying with. He told me Jim spent the night out with friends. This can't be my Jim," she sobbed.

"The Italian authorities have confirmed your son's identity. We can provide you as much detail as possible when our representatives arrive."

"Oh, my God… Oh My God!" Angela cried out between sobs.

"We are so sorry for your loss. Can our representative meet you tomorrow morning at your home, say 10:00 a.m.?"

After a long pause she wiped tears away with the backs of her hands.

"Yes," her voice quivered, "I'll be here."

Angela pressed the "off" button on her phone and placed her head in her hands weeping uncontrollably.

Collecting herself after a few minutes, and still in a period of disbelief, she placed another call to Franco Romano at Bella Ballerina Winery.

"Franco Romano…"

She could hardly believe he picked up the phone after avoiding her calls. She interrupted Romano as soon as he began to speak.

"Franco, this is Angela…why have you not answered my calls?"

"Uh…well…Angela you say?"

"I just received a call from the State Department informing me that Jim is dead! Automobile explosion? Tell me there is some…horrible mistake."

The pause seemed to last for minutes. She stared at the phone and tapped it on the table.

"Franco?"

"I only heard of this a very short time ago. I was told you were being notified by American authorities. I am so sorry, I can't even begin to understand the shock you must feel. It does not seem real to me."

"Franco, someone killed him."

"That is what I was told, as well."

"You must help me get to the bottom of this," she pleaded. "Tony will…"

"Tony, is he free?"

"No, but…"

"I will do what I can, but I wonder if Jim made enemies who would want to harm him? He had a few run-ins here, but Tony implied he had enemies in America."

"Maybe a few malcontents, but no one would do this."

"No one? You know, I will do whatever I can to help you. The bombing is being thoroughly investigated," Romano said before excusing himself from the call.

Though she had suppressed it, the seed Romano planted had crossed Angela's mind. She was aware of the charges that had been brought against Jim in the overdose death of Billy Brewer. Perhaps, someone decided to administer their own form of justice. Maybe that P.I. Tony had mentioned. *What is his name? Fournette?*

With her world crumbling around her, Angela Marasco knew she would need to tell Tony the tragic news of their son's death as soon as she could arrange a meeting.

David was invited by the FBI to sit in as they placed a call to the Italian authorities. Armed with very specific evidence, Alan Smith renewed their contact with the federal Italian military police. U.S. authorities were able to show an uninterrupted chain of events indicating Bella Ballerina Winery was in the business of selling more than wine, olive oil, and balsamic vinegar.

Wired photographs outlined the entire 25i process that took place at the Hammond warehouse including the product in its original balsamic bottles, as well as the bottle transfer process. A precise money trail was also uncovered which outlined the dates payments were made to a shell company owned by Franco Romano.

The Guardia di Finanza had sufficient evidence to move on Romano and shut down his operation. It became even more intriguing that the son of Romano's business partner was recently murdered in Cortona.

When the federal police made their visit to Bella Ballerina Winery, they possessed all the necessary paperwork to fully examine the winery and villa. The timing could not have been worse for Romano and Armand Murati. The Albanian and Romano were caught red-handed as they attempted to move the 25i processing and bottling equipment from the concealed storage facility.

It did not take long for Armand to try saving his own skin by fully implicating Romano as the brains and money behind the operation. The collapse of the international drug operation was complete. The entire Bella Ballerina Winery complex was padlocked and placed under the control of the Italian authorities.

Bella Romano screeched the blue Fiat convertible to a stop in front of the winery.

"What are you doing with my husband?" she pleaded.

"Your husband is under arrest for international drug smuggling. The entire commercial operation is being closed down until his case is adjudicated."

"That is impossible; my husband is a respected wine maker. You are making a grave mistake. Ask the chief of the municipal police; he will tell you. Franco is an honest businessman."

"This is a federal matter, Signora. The municipal police have no jurisdiction in this case."

Everything seemed to fall apart with no warning. The beautiful Italian had no reason to get involved in Romano's business. She only reaped the comforts and rewards. The entire mess seemed like a cruel joke.

Bella wondered what she and the kids would do. She was used to the best, and she enjoyed the adulation she received as the beautiful wife of a powerful man. But now her meal ticket had been carried off to prison.

⚜

When he heard all the details, David tried not to gloat. When everyone else had been willing to drop the case altogether, his persistence and cunning instincts had shut down a drug operation that would have harmed thousands. He had sent two major crime bosses to prison. He had pierced the cocoons of two women across two continents, two women who had lived off the misery of others. No longer would they be allowed to enjoy their many luxuries under the naïve notion that what you don't know can't really hurt you. But most of all, he had brought justice to his family, and against all odds, he had survived.

CHAPTER 26

❧

Angela Marasco loved her husband but she dreaded this meeting. She knew she had to deliver the news of Jim's death in person. She nervously twisted locks of her hair as she and Jeremy Givens waited for the officers to escort the shackled man into the visiting area. She rose to embrace Tony, but he did not respond with any affection. He stood rigid, hands cuffed in front of him.

As they sat back down, Angela broke into tears.

"I'm afraid...I have some terrible news," she sniffled.

"I hear nothing but bad news, for four days now. What? They found more evidence?"

"It's Jim," she sobbed.

"Jim?" Tony shook his head. "What's he done now?"

"He's..." she broke down. "He's....he's dead."

"Dead? Jim? How?"

"His rental car...it...it exploded."

Tony slumped backward in his chair, but remained expressionless. He listened to every word his wife and attorney said, but he just shook his head in disbelief.

"But…what did Franco say?"

"Odd," she said. "He wouldn't return my calls for two days. He said Jim had enemies."

"That bastard! Explosion…you mean a bomb? That son of a…"

"Tony," Givens said, "let's not make any assumptions."

Angela was too distraught to go on. Givens took over and explained how the State Department would help get Jim's body back to the United States. He explained the Italian investigation was continuing, and they would be updated as the names of suspects surfaced. He also informed him that Franco Romano had been arrested.

Shockingly, throughout his discourse, Tony neither moved nor spoke. He seemed in a trance and devoid of emotion. Givens paused and waited for some sign he had actually heard and understood.

Tony slowly looked up as though he would speak.

"Will I be able to attend my son's funeral?"

Angela saw her husband's pale and forlorn expression. She had never seen him react like this. Sometimes he was angry, but he had never before been indecisive or looked so weak.

"It will be up to the judge, Tony," Givens said, almost apologetically.

The now humbled and beaten man shook his head. Like a thunderbolt, the realization seemed to have finally come to Tony Marasco. His ill gotten wealth and power were gone. Now he was like any other punk in federal custody. He faced charges that could keep him confined in a federal penitentiary for the rest of his life. Prospects for bail were remote, and there was no John Gendusa to drag his ass out of the fire. Even Jeremy Givens seemed helpless.

Angela panicked at the thought her life would never be the same.

"Don't give up, Tony," Angela said. "I need you. I feel like I've lost… everything."

"They killed my son, and I have no answers," Tony said rising from his chair.

The once robust and larger than life crime boss now seemed frail and unkempt. Designer suits were replaced by orange jumpsuits. He was only a caricature of the dapper and flamboyant man he once was.

As Tony was being led away from the meeting room in shackles, he turned to Angela and Givens and said something that made little sense to either of them.

"I tried to tell Jim…David Fournette is a dangerous man."

Ironically, the hearings for Tony Marasco and Franco Romano were held on the same day. David was a bit early as he sat in the courtroom for the bail hearing. Brenda was by his side. He felt his cell phone vibrate and took it out of his pocket.

"Hello."

"David, it's Mark."

"Mark, how in the hell are you?"

"All healing nicely, how about you?"

"Cloud nine," David said, "cloud nine. Waiting for the judge now."

"Say, did you hear about Gervais?"

"Lieutenant Ben Gervais…the ultimate a-hole? What about him?"

"He's in the slammer, that's what."

"Are you kidding me? What happened?"

"Bribery. Get this, he was on the take."

"No…Mr. I'm gonna be Police Chief Gervais? So who was payin'?"

"Marasco. Seems Tony was funneling him cash."

"No wonder…that bastard."

"And get this…you're not going to believe this one. They're giving me his job."

"Holy…well, it's about time you got promoted. Talk later…gotta go… Marasco's on his way into the courtroom."

As Tony entered and took a position behind the defendant's table, he exchanged glances with David. There was sorrow in his hollow, dark eyes. But there was no real remorse. David knew he only wanted revenge on the man who crumbled his empire.

Things are right in the world, David thought.

Considering the severity of the charges and the potential for flight risk, the judge denied bail. Tony slumped down and put his forehead on the table. Givens pulled every legal trick in the book, but the judge held firm.

In an Italian courtroom across the Atlantic, the same fate would befall Franco Romano. The Italian judge was known to take a lenient position when charges were brought against rich and powerful people, especially if he could benefit in some way, but Romano's case was different. The combination of national police, federal prosecutors, and a room full of press shined a bright light on the proceedings. Serious charges of international drug smuggling ensured objectivity and sternness. Romano was finished.

David took his victory and the demise of these two organized crime syndicates in stride. *All in a day's work,* he thought. He did feel some satisfaction knowing there was less likelihood another young man would overdose on synthetic drugs and someone like John Cole would be murdered for trying to do the right thing.

There was an odd sense of finality. At times David had wondered if there would ever be a resolution to this fiasco. The odds had not been in his favor. He had been forced to take huge risks with an adversary who had abundantly more resources and power. But his faith and perseverance won in the end.

The Fournettes looked across at Angela Marasco. All the denial and looking the other way was over. She watched sobbing as Tony was led away.

"I feel kinda sorry for her," Brenda said. "I don't exactly know why."

David walked out of the courtroom and into the New Orleans' sunshine with his beautiful wife by his side. *Life is good,* he thought. As they exited the portico, he observed the hastily called press conference on the courthouse steps. Hammond was beaming behind a cluster of microphones. Every local television station was present, even some national press.

"There they are," Brenda laughed, "ready to take credit for quashing the evil Marasco Empire. What a bunch of…"

"They were some help, Bren," David interrupted. "Without them, it would have been harder to bring these people to justice."

"Yeah, right. But only Alan and Mark stuck with you when the going got tough."

The press conference was a real production. Special Agent in Charge Andy Hammond sang the praises of local law enforcement, the prosecutor and the FBI. Just as Alan Smith had predicted, his boss forgot to mention David.

Well, at least Alan's ass is off the hot-seat, David thought.

As was the case at all press conferences convened for public show, the NOPD Chief, federal prosecutor and Assistant Special Agent Smith stood silent and ceremoniously behind the Special Agent in Charge. All were dressed formally in their suits and police attire. They all seemed to enjoy playing the part of heroes.

Only Alan Smith seemed somewhat uncomfortable. He shifted his feet and glanced to his left. He made eye contact with David and Brenda as they were walking past and down the courthouse steps. As Alan caught David's attention, he simply opened his hands and smiled.

Thus David triumphed over the Philistine with sling and stone; he struck the Philistine dead, and did it without a sword in his hand. (First Samuel 17:50)

The End

EPILOGUE

Thanksgiving Day, November 22, 2012 was sunny with temperatures in the low 70's. Living in New Orleans did have benefits. The Fournette family was joined by David's sister, Nancy, and her husband, Tom.

Though Tom and Nancy Brewer still felt a gap in their lives, they had gained some amount of closure knowing those "Marasco murderers" would not inflict similar pain on other parents. Tom filled his days by concentrating on his optometric practice, and they had both returned to golf and tennis at their club. Of course, the wounds would never totally heal, but David felt a sense of peace knowing his sister and brother-in-law had found some degree of enjoyment in their lives.

Rob and Tim were doing quite well in high school and on the baseball diamond, and the trauma of Tim's ordeal had faded into the past. What a tremendous sense of pride David felt. His entire family had stuck by him when there was every reason to do otherwise.

If only adults had the resiliency of teenagers, he thought.

Brenda scurried around the kitchen as she and Nancy put the finishing touches on the Thanksgiving meal. David looked at her with admiration knowing most women would have lost it during the dark days of the kidnapping, but she had remained steadfast. Now, she was the same carefree spirit she had always been. The laughter and banter made it seem like old times.

Tony Marasco's trial was set for January, 2013, and due to the insurmountable evidence and heinous nature of his crimes, it was projected he would remain in the federal penitentiary for a minimum of twenty-five years. Ironically, David had supported Angela Marasco when she asked that her husband be allowed to attend their son's funeral, accompanied, of course, by federal marshals. Though Tony Marasco was an evil man, David felt every father deserved the opportunity to mourn the death of his son.

Franco Romano remained incarcerated in Italy, and his winery was about to be auctioned. The ever resourceful love of his life, Bella, had made the acquaintance of a very rich Italian businessman who, by coincidence, had an interest in the winemaking business. She had every expectation he would succumb to her charms and bid on the winery. The beautiful dancer was prepared to do whatever it took to maintain the lifestyle to which she and her children had become accustomed. After all, what was she to do, when her husband's crimes left them in potential ruin?

Special Agent in Charge, Andy Hammond, was able to parley his good fortune and PR skills into a job at FBI headquarters in Washington DC, proving one could get ahead by playing politics. There was a silver lining. Alan Smith was now the Special Agent in Charge of the New Orleans district office. David knew the promotion was richly deserved. Alan had stood by him and fought for what was right in the face of tremendous opposition. He would always be grateful.

David was amused when Smith told him he didn't know if he had the audacity to deal with all the propaganda and bullshit that came with his promotion.

"You'll do what they all do, Alan. Your job is to represent the FBI; you'll do it with honesty and integrity."

Though David had not sought publicity or engaged in self promotion, it became common knowledge that he was the main cog in eliminating a drug distribution ring across two continents. That was obviously good for business. Messages piled up on his office phone.

Subsequent to the Marasco indictment, David had already closed three substantial cases, and others were under active investigation. He wondered if, at some point, the newly promoted Mark Harris might be ready to join him in the P.I. business. Mark's perseverance and friendship would not be forgotten.

If this keeps up, David laughed to himself, *I might have to hire a receptionist*.

After a peaceful and bountiful Thanksgiving dinner, David and Brenda finished picking up and headed to bed.

"You certainly seem pleased with yourself," she said. "What are you thinking about?"

David looked up at his wife with a mischievous look.

"I have a lot to be thankful for."

"Is that so?" she said. "How good is it?"

"Well, business is booming, and I may soon need an assistant. What do you think? Should I look for a buxom blond or a hot-blooded redhead?"

Glancing over her shoulder, David's confident and sensuous wife gave him a come hither stare.

"Be careful, buster, you already have more than you can handle."

Made in the USA
Lexington, KY
28 August 2013